Summer with a twist

* * *

Citra Tenore

Summer with a Twist

Copyright © 2015 by Citra Tenore.

Email: john@perceptivecomm.com

Cover design by Caitlin Caudill

Ordering Information: Special discounts are available on quantity purchases by corporations, associations, and others. For details, contact the publisher at the email address above.

Tenore / Citra Y. — First Edition

ISBN 978-0-9962016-0-5

Printed in the United States of America

To my fourth and fifth grade English teachers,
Mrs. McCausland and Mrs. Nussbaum, who
encouraged me to press the "Start" button

1

I giddily walk out of the library and shift The City of Bones to my right arm while my eight-year-old brother, Armand, runs in circles around me. Dad takes out his car keys and gives us the usual, "calm down, you two" comment. Armand tries to jump on my back while pretending he's doing a strike from a Pokémon character...Mega EX or something. They're all the same to me. Usually, I would yell at Armand and tell my dad to get him off me. But today, I don't care. I'm just way too giddy because of...of...the concert tomorrow!

It's going to be awesome. Okay, I don't really love the band, but the concert will be a definite blast. I'll be with my friends and I haven't seen half of them all summer. Sarah, Eliza, Adiva, Azra, and me. We'll be going nuts and making total fools of ourselves. That's the fun part. Oh, and about Adiva, yes, I actually have a friend named Adiva, which seems to make people always like "whoa!" when they meet her. I have a feeling it was no coincidence that she was named that, because she is a total diva. We once went on a nature hike, and she wore a puffy, sparkly white skirt with flats. Sarah, Eliza, and Azra aren't really divas. They're all very casual, in a good way. But they have all loved One Direction for as long as I can remember. And tomorrow night's the night...THE night.

It all started one day last month when I was listening to my radio. The top stations were having ticket give-away contests for the One Direction concert. They went on and on about it every time a song finished. I wasn't really thrilled by the songs, but I knew my friends and I would have a blast there no matter what. So we kept calling and trying to win tickets. It was hysterical. We'd get on chats, have screaming five-person phone calls and post silly Instagram pics to prove we were each working hard to win. We failed. Yup, but we had so much fun failing. My parents kept yelling at me to keep it down though.

Less than a week later, I found my dad sitting at his computer when I came home after playing basketball with my neighbors. I remember I tried so many times to see what he was doing, but he wouldn't tell me. He only hinted that it was a surprise. That drove me insane for the rest of the night, since I'm one of those people who DOESN'T like surprises. I literally went crazy trying to figure out what he was doing. But he was so annoyingly laid back, and every time I'd poke my head into his room and beg for an answer, he would just look away and say, "Be patient." But I knew it was something huge, because he never looks at his computer at night. He always says, "I shut down at five, and that's the beauty of being my own boss."

Now I don't like impatient people, because they're always nagging me to get going faster, finish up my breakfast or do my homework before dinner. But the thing is, I'm kind of one of those people sometimes – especially when it comes to secrets or surprises.

So at dinner the next night, Dad finally spilled the beans. He totally fooled me. He looked at me seriously, and in a fatherly tone of voice said, "Chloe, I need to talk to you. I just got off the phone with Sarah's father, and apparently there's a situation with you two and a few of your friends." Suddenly, my head started spinning. "What did he find out?" I asked myself. "Was it the YouTube video with Eliza? But how? She was using a completely random and phony screen name. I mean, it's not super bad or anything. But oh no! There's that one part where we were making fun of Ms. Nestor, our math teacher. I'm dead. Now why's Armand smiling? Does he know? Is he happy I'm finally the one in trouble instead of him? Is Dad angry? He doesn't look it."

Finally he asks, "Why are you turning red?" Even though my head was filled with guilt feelings, I tried to seem casual. I did my best laid back shrug and said nothing. Maybe it's not the video, I thought. I better keep quiet.

"Anyway," he said, "Sarah's parents apparently discovered you and your BFFs…"

"Dad, please don't," I said.

"Fine, you and your friends apparently like this so-called band One Direction. So, Sarah's parents, your mother and I, and some of your other friends' parents have agreed that you can all go to the One Direction concert next month. The tickets have already been bought."

I was speechless. I mean, not only was I not in trouble, I was going out for the night of my life! Like any other 12-year-old girl would be after hearing this kind of news, I went berserk. I literally did jumping jacks around the dinner table and hugged Armand, almost making him choke to death on his chicken sandwich. I was so happy that night I couldn't sleep. And now, I can't even breathe because the weekend is here!

As we get near our car, my dad's phone rings, and he fumbles trying to answer it while pulling out his keys. "Hello?"

Armand reaches the car and struggles to sit on top of the trunk. He's still too short, so I go over and help him up. "What do you mean?" I hear Dad ask. "But we already-" His sentence gets cut off, and he looks sort of flustered. "Eek, must be a problem or something with one of his customers," I whisper to Armand. I try to listen, but all I can hear is a muffled voice coming from the other end.

Dad starts to disagree with the person, but again, gets cut off. "There's gotta be another…yes, but she-" Another muffled answer…sort of like the voices of adults in those Charlie Brown holiday specials, "Mwa-mwa. Mwa-mwa-mwa."

I give up on my eavesdropping and join Armand on the trunk of the car, because the conversation sounds too depressing and doesn't involve me anyway.

Armand unwraps a piece of gum, then whispers, "I don't like it when Dad talks business. It's so boring." Then, he tries to snatch the City of Bones from my right hand, but I don't let him take it. Normally, I have no problem with him checking out one of my books. But the thing is, this one has a picture of some shirtless dude on the front cover.

I don't really want Armand showing my dad, because he'll make me bring it back. And believe me, that's exactly what Armand would do – "Look dad! Chloe's being 'inappropro' again!" He drives me nuts. I hate when he says "inappropro." It reminds me of those snotty elementary school sayings, like "I know you are, but what am I." Besides, I saw the City of Bones movie, and it has absolutely nothing to do with this shirtless guy. And it's not as if I like the cover. In fact, I'm planning to immediately put a picture of a hamster or something over the thing as soon as we get home, because the shirtless dude really is cheesy and gross.

"But do you know how mad she'll be?" Dad asks into the phone. This she person is really making me want to ask him who it is, but I know he'll be mad because it's "none of your business, Chloe."

"Okay, fine," Dad says. "Just don't blame me when she gets all pouty and cries at the drop of a hat all weekend. Yeah, uh-huh, yup. Love you, too." He hangs up and looks over at me.

"Did you just say you loved a business person, Dad?" Armand asks. "And who dropped their hat?" Dad and I look at Armand, but neither of us really feels like explaining. He never listens to the answer when he asks a question anyway.

"Sooo, I was just talking to your mother," Dad says to me. Suddenly, I think this mysterious she they were discussing is me. But why would I be upset? Whatever it is can't be so bad, especially since I'm in such a good mood.

"And you remember that Auntie Heather and Uncle Brygus invited us to their house in Nantucket?" Dad asks.

SUMMER WITH A TWIST

"Yes," I answer, although I had completely forgotten.

"You know how we were supposed to go next week?" he adds.

"Uh huh."

"Okay, well anyway," he says in a weird, guilty voice and kind of squirms. "Well, the thing is, Auntie Heather and Uncle Brygus can't do it next weekend. This is the only possible weekend."

"So, what's that got to do with me?" I reply casually. But I'm starting to boil over inside my head. I'm thinking, "No way. Don't say it. Don't even think it. No, you know what...don't even have a random thought that might lead to a hunch that makes you think it."

But he does. He just quickly blurts out, "Umm, you see...We have to leave at four in the morning for Nantucket, so you can't go to the concert tomorrow."

I drop the book out of my hand and look at my brother, who just bites his nails, then I look back at my dad...I'm speechless.

"I'm sorry," he says. "But your mom really wants this weekend with them. She's already said yes to the invite, and we've been trying to spend time with their family all year. It's just that, as a doctor, Uncle Brygus is always busy and cancelling last minute."

I burst into tears. "Why would she do that to me?!" I ask. "And what about everybody else?! Sarah and those guys, what are we going to tell them?!"

"Keep your voice down," he answers. "They'll be ok. Maybe we should give the extra ticket to one of your friends' sisters or something."

"That's not an extra ticket! That's my ticket! I haven't seen Sarah and Eliza since school ended."

"I can't change this one, Chloe."

"Well, what if I stay with Sarah's family for the weekend? I wouldn't be bothering anyone, and her parents already invited me."

"Your mother says uncle Brygus and Auntie Heather would be offended if you didn't come."

"Offended?" I kind of shake. "But she knows I haven't seen Sarah and Eliza since June, and I won't see them in school this year, because they're switching to that charter school."

"I understand how you feel, but your Mom's word is final."

"But so what if we're going tomorrow? Why can't I come later, like with you or something on Sunday? Let Armand and Mom go ahead of us." I know how dumb that sounded, but I'm desperate.

Dad sighs and looks at me like my IQ just dropped below nine. "Really, Chloe? Break up the family on our one weekend away this summer? That's not an option. Now we have to leave at four in the morning to catch the ferry, which means you have to be up by three. So, let's get out of here, go home and get packed."

I don't move. I cross my arms and just stare at him.

"Now," he commands. He's got that strict fatherly look on his face. I know it's not his fault, so I reluctantly get off the trunk and follow him to the car. But Instead of sitting in front like I usually do, I purposely open and close the front door, slamming it shut. Then I plop myself into the back seat as loudly as I can and sigh as heavily as possible. He glances at me in the rearview mirror but says nothing.

2

Stomping up the stairs, I go into my bedroom and slam the door behind me. Then, I just stand there with my back to the door, waiting for Dad to yell at me for slamming it. I hope he yells at me. That way, I can yell something back. This stupid trip. How can I get out of it? But I know it's no use. I argued the whole way home, and he wouldn't bend at all.

I stand there for ten minutes, imagining all the nasty things I'll say to Mom when she gets home. I may as well pack my clothes and get as ready as I can to face this abominable "vacation".

I open the closet door and step in, grab my bag and lay it on my bed. One more problem. I can't function without my music. So, I go over to my radio, turn it on, and turn the volume up to five. Not too loud and not too quiet. I'd actually prefer it louder, but anything over level five, and Armand will come running in and jump around. He's always looking for an excuse to fling himself into my stuff and mess with it, because he's trashed his room and is jealous of my clean one.

As usual, I start on 103.3. It plays the latest songs that my generation likes. I basically know every song by heart, even the ones I hate. I walk over to my tee-shirt drawer and grab my track and field shirt, my long white one, and the red shirt that says "Grade 6 Rules!" on the back. Weaving inside and around the slogan is everyone's name from my sixth grade class. And oh yeah, like it or not, I'll be off to school soon. In two weeks and two days, to be exact.

I fold each of the shirts and put them in my travel bag, then I grab a fistful of underwear, because who knows how many pairs of those I'll need. I put them in the bag. I always make sure to place my underwear in between my other clothes so that no one can see that they're there. Two years ago, my family went to Florida, and I had to get changed after my shower. I had packed my underwear on the top layer, and Armand ran around yelling that he saw it. "I saw Chloe's undies! I saw Chloe's undies!" So immature. Okay, maybe he was only six at the time. But he was so loud that I'm sure the people in the rooms around us heard him. Besides, seriously, like I never see his?

I go to my other drawer and grab three pairs of shorts; one yellow, one blue, and one that's white with black stripes and kind of looks like zebra pajamas.

Here's my straight advice about zebra-striped clothing: Don't wear zebra-striped shorts to school. It'll take two months to stop hearing all the dumb jokes about it. The kids were so immature: "Hey Chloe, where you going in those shorts – Madagascar? What's black-white-yellow, black-white-yellow? Chloe watching the buses leave the school!" Ha-ha-ha. Whatever. Boys are such idiots. Which brings me back to my biggest fear about this weekend. Boys. Lots of boys.

I'm sure tons of older people and girls my age would ask, "Hey Chloe, why don't you want to go to Nantucket? People everywhere are dying to go to that island. You get to go there with all the beaches and boats, and you're bummed out about it? Are you crazy?" Not trying to sound spoiled, but I'm literally going to be the only girl on this trip.

Vacation? This is no vacation for me. Five boys against one girl is a nightmare. So, here's the list of people I'm going to be sharing my nightmare and un-private, teeny-weenie space with from Saturday to Monday:

<u>The Germanos Family</u>

- Hunter. He's thirteen.
- Cerel. He's twelve, like me. But way more sarcastic…and annoying.
- Faegan. Another boy. Age ten.

- Dominic. Yet another boy. Age eight and crazy out of control.
- Baby Sara. Almost two. She's a little cutie, but obviously, no help to me.
- Uncle Brygus (the dad). He isn't really my uncle, but we just say that.
- Auntie Heather (the mom). Again, she isn't really my aunt.

My Family, the Taliris
- Me (Chloe Taliri).
- Armand (my brother). He's eight. But worse, he acts like an idiot whenever Dominic's around, which will be all weekend.
- Dad (John)
- Mom (Ria)

Seriously, I'm gonna be the only girl there who doesn't wear diapers. Mom and Auntie Heather don't really count as girls either. They don't understand what girls need and they never do anything when the boys get annoying or start trying to burn stuff or blow up stuff. THREE days of this and nowhere to hide.

The thought gets me sweating mad again. I angrily pluck a pair of yoga pants from my closet along with a purple pullover sweater. Then I go over to my sock drawer and grab six pairs, because I'm one of those people who gets really uncomfortable being barefoot. I don't know why. I guess it just freaks me out that I might step on something nasty, like a dead bug or bird poop. I won't even go barefoot in my own yard during the summer unless I'm on a Slip-and-Slide.

The song on the radio changes to Problem. Yes, I have a pretty big problem right now – trapped with five boys on an island for a long weekend while my friends make awesome memories without me. This song pretty much sums it up for me.

After packing my clothes into my bag, I realize that I can't be stranded on Nantucket with nothing to read. I go over to my book shelf and pull out my copy of The Hunger Games to bring with City Of Bones. The Hunger Games is my backup book.

I read it whenever one of my borrowed books turns out to be so boring that I just have no interest in seeing what happens after five pages. I decide not to cover the picture of the shirtless dude on City of Bones. He can help me get some revenge on Mom. After all, if she didn't want to see some inappropriate, shirtless cheeseball on my book, then she should have left me and the book home with my friends.

I throw the books into the clothing bag, then go into the bathroom I share with Armand. I grab a small red bag and put all my soap related stuff in it, since I'm gonna need it for showering. I zip this up, go back to my room and find the perfect spot to squeeze it into my clothing bag. As I go to zipper that up, the zipper grabby thing snaps off in my hand. Great. A broken zipper at the very end, and it's not closing. I kick the bed out of frustration and hit my toe. Ow!

Rolling around on my bed in pain, all I can see are purple and blue dots swirling in the air as my eyes look up toward the ceiling. After a few minutes, the pain starts to go away, and I can focus my vision again. Staring at the ceiling, it looks really boring to me. Plain white. How come it's so dull? I should put something up there. For now, I just shift my focus to the walls.

My bedroom walls are painted purple - a happy color. I stare at them while I rub my toe, and the pain seems to flow out of my body through the end of my foot. Hmm, that's surprising. I wonder how that happens. Maybe it's the colors and the stuff on my walls. Pretty soothing. The wall next to my bed has a poster of Katniss from The Hunger Games. She's standing, ready to shoot, in the middle of her mocking jay pin. The top of the poster reads: Remember who the real enemy is. Oh, I remember. It's my parents. They're making me do this. They're the ones who killed my entire night.

I try to think of a happy memory. That way I don't end up depressing myself about my anger towards my parents. Ah, here's a good memory: Halloween last year. I was Bellatrix Lestrange for Halloween and got tons of weird looks. Like, what's going on people? Haven't you ever seen

Harry Potter? The snake and skull tattoo probably had something to do with the weird looks. But finally one girl, who I think was seventeen or eighteen, recognized that I was Bellatrix. She made my night by quoting one of Bellatrix's lines. My friends also liked the costume, which was good to hear for my dad, considering how hard he worked on it. He actually rolled around in charcoal dust with the prisoner pants and shirt on so they'd look grimy and blotchy like Bellatrix.

The radio channel goes to commercial and gets interrupted by my mother yelling "Hello!" to the entire house. She does that all the time. There'll be no one around, and she'll just walk in and scream her head off until someone comes. I'll be in the middle of doing a math problem. "Let's see...one-fourth times three-fifths divided by seven-eighths is....HELLOOOOOOO!!!!!" Then, I have to start the problem all over again.

Well, I'm starving, and she probably brought home food like she does every Friday after work. So, I shut off the radio, turn off my bedroom lights, and head down the stairs. I might be super mad at her, but my stomach is getting super mad at me for not eating all afternoon. My personality is "hangry", as I learned from one of my friends. The definition is: the state of being both angry and hungry at the same time.

"Hi Chloe!" Mom yells way too happily. I try ignoring her as I enter the foyer, but she squeezes me like she's a juicer machine and I'm an orange. "I'm so excited about going to Nantucket! It's going to be so much fun at the beach!"

"Mmm," I reply. So rude of her. How can you completely ruin my weekend and then come in all smiley and bubbly? I'm about to say something sarcastic, but she quickly rushes into the family room to give my brother a hug, then she goes upstairs to shower.

I actually know why she's acting all super happy. It's because she loves beaches more than anything in the world. She grew up in the mountains and could never go to the beach as a kid. Every time we're looking for ideas for something to do on a boring summer day, she tries to steer us toward the nearest beach.

After gulping down some pizza Mom brought home, I sit on one of the high chairs at the island in our kitchen. They're not baby high chairs, just those spinney chairs you see at fun restaurants. There's a diner with a jukebox music player near our home, and it has these same chairs at the counter. I start fiddling with the watermelon slices in front of me. They are sliced just right so that I can make them rock back and forth when I softly tap one end with my pinky finger. As I do, I can hear the weird noises from my brother's Mario Kart Wii that he got for his birthday.

My dad enters the kitchen and plugs in the coffee machine. "Why do we have to go this weekend?" I ask, making a final attempt to change his mind. "I mean, why do I have to go? I could sleep at Adiva's and Sarah's all weekend. Their parents said it was okay."

"Um, we already went over this. We're staying together as a family," he says while scanning the cabinet for a coffee mug. "We're going on vacation, and Auntie Heather and Uncle Brygus have prepared a lot for us to come over." He flips open the coffee machine, pours coffee beans into it, then turns around to look at me. "And I think you're going to have a great time…?"

The fact that he drifted off from his sentence and turned it into a question means that he also knows I'm going to have a cruddy time.

"You should prepare tonight, because you won't wanna pack in the morning," he says.

"I already packed my bag."

"Good, but don't over-pack."

I spin the watermelon. Huh, I didn't know it could spin so fast. "But Dad, the only thing a girl who's going to be stranded on an island with five idiot boys can do is over-pack, because she knows that there will be nothing to do and she needs her stuff to survive."

"Hmph," he mutters and pours his coffee. Without another word, he walks into the sunroom and leaves me sitting alone in the kitchen.

3

Someone is shaking me really violently and yelling. "Chloe, wake up! Wake up! We don't want to miss the ferry!" I thrash my arm and hit something, actually, someone's neck. I open my eyes to find my mom standing over me. "Finally!" she says. "Now get your clothes on and bring your stuff down when you're ready." She walks out of the room.

"Huh? What?" I whisper. I nod "yes". Why am I nodding? No one's here. But that's how much of a morning person I'm not. My brain barely sends signals to my body on weekend mornings, especially at three in the morning.

"Get UP!!!!" Mom screams from the bottom of the stairs. I drag myself out of bed, and my feet touch the floor. What the-?! Freezing! Of course, at three in the morning everything is cold, even in the summer. The earliest I ever got up this summer was eight. That's probably not a good thing, since we're going to have to be at school by seven-thirty this coming fall.

I kind of crawl out of bed and just slide into the bathroom, shut the door behind me and splash water onto my hands and face without even daring to look in the mirror. I never like to look at myself when I wake up, because my hair's a wreck. I go back into my bedroom and turn on the radio. It plays Chandelier. It's a calm but loud song -- pretty good for waking up.

I stop myself once I look down at my foot. The second toe has a huge bruise. Actually, it has lost all of its normal skin tone and is completely greenish-blue, with purple dots all around my toenail. The purple dots freak me out. Gross. I pull on a pair of my black yoga pants and a tee-shirt from my grandmother that has a panda sleeping on it. The shirt reads: I don't do mornings. At least

Grandma knows me well. I wish she were coming with us.

I grab my bags and head downstairs. Surprisingly, they're light for once. I drop them by the front door and untie my sneakers so that I don't have to do it when we're about to leave. I don't know why, but I hate untying and tying them all at once. It seems faster and so much easier just slipping my feet into them on the way out the door.

When I walk into the kitchen, I see my dad making coffee like he does every morning. Armand's munching on a Pop Tart while sitting on the floor, and Mom is nowhere to be seen.

"'Morning, Chloe. Beautiful sunrise coming on soon," my dad says to me without looking up from the coffee machine. He's obviously trying to make me see the bright side.

"Hmph," I mumble quietly. Dad grabs a nearby mug and puts it under the machine. When the coffee comes down, it sounds like someone's peeing. Yuck. And it takes so long. Why can't the coffee just splash out fast the way it does at soda fountains?

"Goo-Goo," my brother says to me. Even though he's already eight, he likes to embrace the fact that he's the baby of the family. I just stare down at him from my chair. He's wearing the blue ninja shirt he slept in last night. Well, technically, it is still last night, so I guess it's not so bad.

"We're leaving in twenty minutes," Dad says as he turns around to look at us. He takes a sip of his coffee and gives a strange look towards Armand who is now spinning around in circles. Sometimes Armand is annoying when he acts little, and other times he's funny. As he whirls around with his wild hair and huge smile, he looks kinda funny.

"I haven't had breakfast yet," I tell my dad.

"I know," he says. "That's why I bought a bunch of food last night for the car ride."

"How long's the car ride?" I ask. He takes a long sip of his coffee before saying anything.

Oh no. I knew I shouldn't have asked. Whenever he takes a long sip of his coffee before answering a question, it means the answer's going to be painfully detailed. "We have to drive down to Hyannis," he says. "That will take an hour. Then we get on the ferry, and that'll take two hours, assuming there are no delays. Then, once we get there, I have no idea. So…three or four hours."

I groan. I'm being dragged on a four-hour journey? Why isn't there some sort of plane ride for this?

Mom enters the kitchen from the dining room, holding her computer. "So the website shows that the ferries are running on time," she says. "We need to leave in ten minutes." Then she looks at me, "Can you get two pillows, one for your brother and one for you? Thanks."

"Sure," I say flatly, and I can see she knows I'm over this. But she'll just ignore me. I walk up the stairs two at a time. I can't stand climbing stairs when I'm sleepy, and I figure going two at a time will mean less work. Still, it feels like forever. I reach my parents room, take two of their long pillows and hug them to my face as I walk back downstairs. I could fall asleep in these.

This always happens. We have to leave in ten minutes, and the mad scramble has started. My parents and brother run around the house looking for their clothes. Armand rolls his Toy Story suitcase into the kitchen and tries to stuff practically all the clothing he owns into it. Way too small. My dad runs into the basement and comes back up with two shirts and a pair of pajama pants with Stewie from Family Guy on them. I got him those for his birthday a few years ago. He laughed when he first saw them. But it turned out badly when Mom wanted to know how I, who was only eight years old back then, knew that Stewie was the funniest character on the show. I wasn't allowed to even know about the show. But having a favorite character, uh-oh.

It was actually worse for my dad than for me, because Mom blamed him for it. Dad is a little stricter now and pokes his head into the family room whenever he hears us change the channel. As for me, I just play dumb and don't buy gifts with TV show characters on them anymore. I tried to warn Armand, but last month he went and spit out to my parents how he loves South Park. Let's just say I got to play with his Wii all by myself for a week. I warned him.

I sit at the kitchen table, sipping a cup of tea and watching them scramble everywhere to find their clothes. Well, at least my parents are scrambling. Armand has given up on packing. He's now crawling by my feet, wearing his Superman underwear on his head and making baby sounds again.

"Armand!" my mom screams at him. She starts yelling about how she has to do everything for him and clean for him and wash his clothes and then something about how he has to grow up and be ready for college one day. He looks up and stares with big puppy eyes half-full of tears. He's such a faker, but Mom totally falls for it.

It's the same thing every time. He does something idiotic. She starts screaming. He puts on the baby pout. She picks him up, hugs him and says something about him being so cute and cuddly…blah, blah, blah. It's very interesting to just watch my family live. Kind of like they're a different species or something. Actually, I know that my brother is a different species.

I finish drinking my tea and put the cup in the sink. I start to head upstairs to brush my teeth, but Mom stops me in the hallway. "Are you sure you packed everything?" she asks. I nod.

"Underwear?"

"Yes."

She stares at me. "Shirts, pants, shorts, undershirts, and sweatshirts?"

"Yeeeeeess," I say, completely frustrated.

"After another minute of our constant "what about this" and "what about that," I finally escape and run upstairs.

4

Armand sits in the back row, which means I get the whole middle row to myself, while my parents sit in the front. The good thing about our SUV is that it isn't like our old minivan. Here, the middle row seats are so high that they block my view of Armand behind me. He's always incredibly hyper on car rides. Even on the short rides to the center of town, he starts tapping his fingers and playing 'off the wall' with a tennis ball on the back of Dad's seat.

I take the small bag with my books and flip it upside down so that I can see everything that's inside it: My two books, some hair accessories and two packs of natural gummy bears. I pick up the two gummy bear packages and turn around to speak to Armand.

"Armand?" I ask. He looks up from reading what looks like MY DIARY. But it's okay, it's my electronic Password Journal that I used until I was ten…nothing too serious in there. "You know I can see the lightning bolts of your underwear through those white shorts?"

"What?" he answers without looking up.

I wave one of the gummy packages in his face. "You want one?"

His face lights up. "YEAHHHH!!!" he screams.

I throw the package over the seat, and he snatches it up fast. Then he scrunches up his legs between his arms and starts rocking back and forth.

"Umm... okay…," I say as I raise an eyebrow.

"Chloweeeee?" he asks in his baby voice. "Can you open the packwage?"

I take back the tiny bag, open it and hand it back. The fruity scent bursts out. He sniffs deeply then jumps up and down in his seat. "Armand!"

SUMMER WITH A TWIST

Mom yells at him. "Put your seat belt on right now!" He puts it on just as Dad starts the car.

"Nantucket, here we come," Dad says. Then, "Chloe, I need one of those chocolate muffins from the food bag."

I open up the bag, take out the muffin container and reach for a chocolate muffin. Once I feel it in my hands with its warm chocolate chunks and squishy bottom, I see why he has a serious need for it. I become almost hypnotized by the chocolaty warmth and think about taking a huge bite. But I can feel him staring at the muffin, practically drooling over the car seat. So I hand it over, but it's really hard not swiping a taste. He snatches the muffin, swings back into his driving position, and bounces up and down like Armand just did. Clearly, it's genetic. Finally, the car starts to move.

Mom keeps going on and on about how the beaches in Nantucket are much better than the ones here in northern Massachusetts and how much exercise and fresh air she's going to get this weekend. Ah, news flash: We live next to a state forest. We pretty much get all the fresh air and exercise a human could ever need. But I don't say anything. I'm still mad at her for making me miss the concert and all my friends, but I'm way too tired to fight about it right now.

"Did you know that you can see the fish there?" she asks, not really looking at any of us. "And it's so peaceful that you'll want to take so many walks! Oh, and you won't get sick of it, because Heather says her kids all enjoy it so much every day! And she says that they live so close to the beach that they can walk to it! And Hunter's on the biology team at the library, and she told me that…"

I look into the food bag and notice another chocolate muffin. Yes! I grab it quickly and quietly. As soon as I bite into it, all voices and sounds in the car sort of melt away behind the extreme chocolate happiness that takes over my brain. It's like I flew a million miles away and landed in chocolate heaven. I have no idea what's happening on earth while I look deeply into the little holes of my muffin. I finish it and feel completely satisfied, like everything will be okay for the first time in twelve hours. I stare out my window and watch the sun coming up from a distance. It's very peaceful viewing the sun from chocolate heaven, and I soon fall asleep.

I wake up as if somebody just slapped me. I'm so startled but can't figure out what happened. I look behind me, and Armand is still reading my old diary. My parents are talking about jobs and schools on islands and how good ones can be hard to find. I definitely napped at the right time. I look out the window to find the sun is up. So, I take out my hair brush and tug it through my tangled hair, which I then turn into a braid.

"Oh! You're awake!" my dad exclaims as if I've just recovered from a coma in the hospital.

"Where are we?" I ask him.

He smiles. "We, my friend, are in Hyannis. We only have about ten more minutes until we need to park our car and get to the ferry from Cape Cod to Nantucket."

Suddenly and out of nowhere, Armand flings my diary over the seat. "Hey! You almost hit me!" I yell at him. "What was that fo-?"

"It's boring!" he says, then he falls onto his pillow without another word.

Dad turns the car into a huge parking lot with a sign that says "Ferry Shuttle Parking." After he parks, we get out and unload our bags. I take out my main bag, which has a dog design on it. It's a cute little puppy with big floppy ears, so that's the side that I let everyone see. I put my smaller bag around my left shoulder, then I help Armand and his Toy Story bag out of the car. "Your diary's boring," he tells me again. "It's all about you being worried about the science fair and stuff. I thought you wrote that in third grade. You're a nerd."

"But I never gave you permission to read my diary, did I?" I throw it back at him, but all he does is try to suck on my arm. Yes, suck on my arm. My brother is THE weirdest person in the history of weird.

Last year, I woke up one Saturday morning with my arm feeling wet as it hung off the side of my bed. When I looked over at it, there was Armand. He was just sitting there sucking on my arm. It turns out he likes the taste of salty skin. That was nothing. Every time my Dad comes in from running or mowing the lawn, Armand goes up to him and tries to suck his arm or lick his cheek. It's horrifying.

Armand laughs as I playfully smack his cheeks and mutter how naughty he is. It doesn't hurt him, because his cheeks are so chubby. They're not fat. They're just chubby the way a baby has chubby cheeks. They're really quite firm. My parents are always hugging my brother, because his body and face are so comfy to squeeze. We have completely opposite genes. He got my Mom's and I got my Dad's. Armand's cute and round-faced like Mom, and I'm long and lean like Dad. I mean, I can't eat everything I want and stay healthy, but I don't have to be as careful as Mom and Armand are. I think it's weird how genetics choose how you look and act sometimes. Strange.

"There it is," My dad says. He's looking to his right, so the rest of us do. And sure enough, the shuttle is coming our way, very slowly. Finally it comes to a stop, and the door opens. The elderly man driving peeks out. "Hey there!" he yells to us. "Going to the islands?"

"Yes sir," my dad replies, and we all hop in. It's pretty full in the shuttle. We put our bags on the racks then follow my dad to the last row of seats.

5

The shuttle bus driver won't stop talking. It's as if we're on a travel tour, but a really boring one. I had fun when my class took a field trip to the Salem Witch museum and listened to the bus driver tell spooky tales of hangings and dungeons as we passed old brick buildings and triangle-shaped wooden buildings that reminded me of witches hats. Even though this driver is really old and nearly scrapes a bunch of cars with the side of the bus, he's a non-stop chatterbox.

Now, I don't have anything against chatterboxes, because that's what most of my friends are. But this...this is unbelievable. He starts droning on about how Cape Cod used to be nicer and how his grandparents ran a fishing supply shop and knew everyone in town. Then, it all changed, and it's just tourists shuttling off to Martha's Vineyard and Nantucket. Gee, doesn't he have a job because of us tourists? What's he complaining about?

I start biting my fingernails out of frustration. I spit a nail out of my mouth, and Mom gives me a grim look. I'm always being told to not bite my nails because it's bad for me and gives a bad impression to others. I have to agree with all that, but the thing is, this man is so annoying that I just can't stop myself. I lean forward and look over at Dad. He's about to lose his mind.

"I can't take this anymore," he says pretty loudly. "We're getting out and walking at the next stop." Mom protests because of our big bag, but Dad says he doesn't care and that he'd rather get the exercise. I mean, the driver just won't stop talking.

To my relief, he stops the bus in a second parking lot and says, "Okay, we're halfway there and just picking up some more tourists."

Practically everyone instantly jumps up, takes their bags and starts to leave the bus. I guess we're not the only ones who are losing it. Two families with little babies stay seated but give us jealous looks. I feel bad for them.

As I jump down onto the pavement from the high step, I hear one guy who just left the bus say to the people waiting to get on, "Good luck. Hope you brought your earplugs." We all laugh. It's pretty fun walking with that group to the ferry terminal. My parents get to have some laughs with the sarcastic guy, while Armand and I throw around a tennis ball with four other kids.

Once we get in line at the ferry terminal, I take The City of Bones out of my bag and flip it open quickly so that no one sees the front cover. Oh, who am I kidding? How am I going to read in a place where people are flying around like bees in a hive? I stuff the book back into my bag and give out a little sigh.

A boy who looks about a year younger than me walks up to the couple in front of us. I'm guessing he's their son, because it would be strange to have some kid just walk up to you and start speaking as if he knows you. He's holding a leash, and my eyes trail down to where the dog is. It's really adorable. I stare at it for a minute, and the dog starts sniffing my leg, and I laugh because it tickles. The boy looks up and smiles, and the couple gives out little laughs. "Is he or she a labradoodle?" I ask them. "I see the little curls and I was just wondering."

"Yes he is," The woman says to me with a smile. My dad gets down to the dog's height and pats the little darling, which starts wagging its tail. Armand smiles, and my mom tries to, but every time the dog steps near her, she gasps. Mom isn't very fond of dogs, and neither was I, until I was nine years old. I now see that dogs are just livelier than cats, and they feel protective of their owners. That makes me feel safe. Safe and happy.

We stand in line and wait…and wait…and wait, until the gates finally open and we're allowed to board the ferry. Dad tries to hand his tickets to some lady by a fence who is wearing a ferry jacket, but she doesn't take them. Instead, she just points to the ferry. Geez, Dad paid more than a hundred dollars, and nobody even checks the tickets. Not that I'm dishonest or anything, but doesn't that mean people can just sneak on without paying?

We're about to walk onto the boat when Mom stops to talk to a few men working in the baggage area. "John!" she yells. "Bring our bags over here."

"What?" Dad says, clearly frustrated. "I could've held onto them. Why did you ask them if-"

"The rules, sir," one of the guys says like an army general. "You have to leave your bags over here."

Dad mutters something about how we shouldn't have wasted our time talking to them about baggage stuff so that we wouldn't have to go through some big crowd when we get off the boat later. Lucky me. I don't have to leave my bags here, because they're both small enough to fit under a seat on the boat.

The first floor of the boat is packed with kids playing games, adults chatting, babies crying, and teens on their phones. That reminds me, I don't have a phone yet and I'll need one for after-school stuff. And ever since I jokingly told my dad that there are phones with just '911' and 'Home' buttons, he's been determined to get me one of those. Of course, I hope to get a smartphone this year. So, I try to stay on my best behavior and hope I don't get stuck with a humiliating 'emergency only' phone.

I follow the rest of my family up the stairs to the second level, and eventually we find four seats in the middle row. My dad goes through first and sits next to a woman who seems pretty old. Armand was about to go first, but he's scared of sitting near strangers, even when my parents are around. He sits next to my dad, then immediately unzips Dad's computer bag.

Of course, Armand is always playing on the computer. It drives me nuts, because he's never reading or anything (unless it's my diary which is, apparently, "boring"). But at least it keeps him out of my hair. Mom goes through next and sits beside Armand, then I go. I'm glad to be sitting on the edge, so if I have to use the bathroom, I don't need to ask anyone. I can just slip out quietly and avoid any embarrassing discussions.

"I forgot to tell you," my dad says looking at all of us. "I didn't know it, but we booked tickets for the one-hour ferry. So, we'll only be on this thing for an hour." That's good, because I don't know if I get sea sick or not.

I open up The City of Bones and start reading, but I get interrupted by my stomach flipping upside down. Or at least, it feels like my stomach is flipping upside down. Am I already sea sick? It's only been what, five minutes? If I'm going through another fifty-five minutes of this, I may come off this boat feeling and looking completely awful.

I close my book and put it back in my bag, then sit here with nothing to do. Looking over at Dad, he's fast asleep. Armand's playing on Dad's phone, and Mom's snoozing. With my stomach feeling queasy, I take the tablet out of the computer bag and open the Internet. In the search bar, I type in *how to prevent being seasick*. I click on one of the search results and read part of the article, then go through the list and read more. But there's one glaring problem. All the advice is about what you should do BEFORE your trip to avoid getting seasick. The first one says, "Eat a big meal the night before and just a small breakfast the day of travel." That stinks. Stupid websites. That didn't help at all. They also say to walk barefoot on your way to the boat. Huh? Are they saying that I should go barefoot throughout the town of Hyannis?

Now my stomach hurts…a lot. I take in a few deep breaths and open a new tab on the computer so I can play a song on YouTube. I try to think of a happy one that might make me feel relaxed. But I can't think of anything. Even if I did pull up a good song, I just realized I didn't bring my ear buds. I close the internet, then put the tablet back into my dad's computer bag. Sigh. I miss my friends.

At least I had fun with some new girls I met in my film acting class last week in Boston. It was kind of a bummer when that week ended. It went by so fast. I did a scene with a girl named Laura. Her twin sister, Lauren, was there too. I know – twins Laura and Lauren – they're really nice. I also made a friend whose name is Isis, like the Greek goddess. Even though she's fifteen, four years older than me, we got along very well. Whenever someone did a good job in one of our scenes, she would say, "Wow! Your acting is smooth like a latte!" Smooth like a latte – good one. It was an exciting week.

I liked traveling into the city every day. It made me feel more mature. Plus, getting to talk with real casting directors and actors who've been in movies was a huge thrill. It felt really strange and boring back home when the week was over, like I had lived in this far away and strange land. Dad says it's only 26 miles from home. Still, my hometown suddenly feels like a tiny rural village when I compare it to the cool events and action happening in the city.

I wonder if I'll ever see my city friends again. It's weird – almost feeling like I betrayed my best friends back home by making new ones and completely focusing on my city life.

My stomach flips like a pancake again, so I get up to use the bathroom. I stumble around looking for it and then…duh, it was right behind me the whole time. I walk in and close the door behind me. Finally. But just as I'm about to sit down, I see a bunch of orange throw-up in the toilet. Oh. My. God. Gross, ew. I guess somebody beat me to it. I rush to the door and open it, then I walk fast back to my seat. Suddenly, I realize that the smell is going to come out of the bathroom and out to where the passengers are. So now, it's all up to me to fix this mess that I didn't even create! I hold my breath and walk back to the bathroom door. The smell has already spread to the opening, so I immediately pull it shut.

People say that if you ever have to breathe bad air, breathe from your mouth. I think that's disgusting, because (a) it feels like the gross germs are entering your system, and (b) you look like a dog. I walk back to my seat and sit down. My stomach only feels worse now that I saw that barf. I'm just about to close my eyes when I hear crash, ding, and vroom! I look to my right and find Armand playing on the phone with the volume on high. "Armand!" I snap, and he looks up. "Turn that thing-"

"Attention…(crackle-crackle)… passengers," The voice from the speaker above my head says. "We will be arriving…(crackle-crackle) … at Nantucket in five minutes. Again, we… (crackle-crackle)…will be… (crackle-crackle)…arriving in Nantucket in five minutes."

People get up and start forming a line behind by the back door. They really seem to rush to get there like it's a race to be first, so I'm thinking it must be important. I turn to my mom and shake her. She wakes up.

"Are we there yet?" she asks me. I nod.

Armand turns to my dad. "DAD! WAKE UP!" and punches him all up the side of his arm. Dad looks ripping mad, grabs Armand's hand and just gives him a death stare. Armand giggles, while

Mom lovingly squeezes his chubby cheeks and tries to hush him because of the people around us. "I have to pee," Armand announces.

Still angry at being awoken that way, Dad ignores Armand and grabs the computer bag. "Daddy," Armand says urgently. "I have to pee." But Dad keeps on ignoring him and just speaks to Mom. "Ria, don't forget that we still have to get our other bags from the checked baggage area."

An employee wearing a blue hat with a gold anchor emblem opens the back door, and people start flooding off the boat fast, as if the thing is on fire. We're about to walk out when Armand begs my dad, "I have to peee-yeeeeeee."

Dad finally looks down at him. "Fine," he says and steers Armand toward the bathroom while Mom and I wait on the back deck.

The employee walks towards us. "Ma'am," he says to Mom. "We're going to have to ask you to disembark now." Who's the "we" he's talking about? I don't see another employee with him.

Mom seems a bit surprised. "But my husband and son are using the bathroom," she says to him.

"I assure you, they'll be fine," the man says. So Mom goes down the stairs, but I stay put. "Please go with your mom, little one," he says to me.

Little one? Now I'm not going anywhere. I just look at him defiantly. He stares back for a second, then seems to realize that he just messed up by calling me that.

He sighs and says, "Sorry. Would you, MISS, please disembark as well with the other mature ladies?"

"Why yes. I'd love to," I reply. But just as I agree, the bathroom door pops open, and Armand runs smack into the guy from behind. He grumbles. We leave the boat...rather, disembark, as they say on Nantucket.

6

Dad, Armand and I find Mom waiting for us by our big pile of bags.

"Is Auntie Heather picking us up here?" I ask Dad.

He fiddles with his phone and opens up his recent text messages. "She says we should walk to The Bean café and meet her there. Apparently, we can ask any local where it is, because everyone who lives here knows about it."

I follow my family through the parking lot and onto the sidewalk. The sun beats down on my dark hair and feels hot on my skin. Already, I feel the sweat trailing down my neck. Man, Mrs. McGrath, my health teacher, was right when she warned us about the sweat. I can't believe it. Mom used to yell at me to shower, and I would think, "Why is she so obsessed with showering? I don't even sweat." But now I'm begging to shower every few hours each day, because I can't stand how disgusting it feels. What's worse is this Nantucket sun is even hotter than back home.

Dad asks some guy where The Bean is, and the guy tells him that it's a fifteen-minute walk into the center of town. Fifteen minutes?! I'll be a puddle of sweat by the time we get there. We walk past a few stores and are just several steps away from the front of a bike shop, when suddenly this super aggressive sales dude comes running towards my dad. "Hi, sir! Would your family like to rent some-?"

"No." my dad says.

"Are ya sure y-?"

"Yes," Dad adds and doesn't stop walking.

I love how my dad just shuts down those sales guys. They're always bugging me and my friends when we walk through the mall. I just can't say no the way Dad does it. Anyway, we keep struggling through the summer heat with our bags, then we take a right corner and Dad stops. I can feel my hair is already starting to frizz even though it's in a braid.

Dad leaves us for a second and goes into a restaurant to ask where The Bean is. I feel really embarrassed. We look homeless walking around Nantucket's busy center with our bags and everything. Because it's not like we just carry a few bags. We're the worst family at packing, so we always bring this mega-huge bag that we have to drag. Plus, Mom sneaks in extra food bags right from the grocery store. They're not like luggage. They're like…nasty grocery food bags with stuff always sticking out the top. If any kid from my school saw me like this, I'd probably die.

Dad comes back with a map of the town. "The lady in the shop said to take two lefts then a right."

We follow Dad through the streets of Nantucket. More sweat. But, I have to admit, it's a very cute center. I like the brick sidewalks instead of cement and how there are no doors to any of the shops. They're just open. At least, I like the town at first. But hauling heavy bags on brick and cobble-stone streets for twenty minutes in summer heat does things to your body and brain, and I quickly start to dislike it as sweat droplets run down my sides.

FINALLY, we reach The Bean and stand out front. Even though Auntie Heather told us that she was there, she isn't. I sit on a nearby bench and wipe the sweat off my face. I wish I could do the same for my legs and feet. Armand sits beside me and starts fiddling with his bag.

"I'm gonna call her," Mom announces. She dials the number into her phone. "Hello? This is Ria. Hi Heather. So we're at The Bean and we don't see you. No...no...yes...no. Okay. Okay. Ya. All right. Got it. Bye!"

"Okay," Mom says, looking at us and clearly feeling proud for some reason. "Auntie Heather says that she's at the place that used to be called The Bean. She says they changed the name a few years ago, but nobody told her about it. She's where the old one was, not this one."

"That makes a lot more sense," Dad says. But he looks pretty annoyed, because of course, he's the one who has to carry the mega-bag. Plus, we find out that The Bean is all the way back to where our boat docked at the ferry landing. Seriously, we just walked through what felt like half of Nantucket in hot summer heat, only to find that we didn't have to walk at all.

Auntie Heather lets out a gasp. "Chloe, you're so tall! You're as tall as you're mom. And you really look like your dad now!" I smile and give her a hug. She's a nice lady and always greets her guests kindly. "Armand!" Auntie Heather says to him. "You're so big now, too! Dominic's in the car waiting for you."

Armand and Dominic sit in the back row by themselves. "What type of Minecraft do you have?" Dominic asks. "OH!" Armand says. "I have the…" I stop listening to their conversation.

The thing is, I know the guys who made Minecraft are millionaires and congrats to them, but could somebody please explain to me why that game is so popular? I've gone over this a bunch of times with people, and I still don't get it. So what? You move a bunch of blocks around and kill zombies. There really isn't much to it.

"So your house is actually right at the beach?" my mom asks with amazement.

"No, but it's only a mile away, and the boys like to bike on the path that leads to it," answers Auntie Heather. "Chloe, we have an extra bike, so you can ride there with Hunter and Cerel.

"Oh… umm," is all I can think to say and give a weak smile. I don't really want to ride a bike with her kids because, well...it's just kind of weird since they're all boys and I don't really know them. But I just ignore the thought for a moment, hoping that she doesn't bring it up again.

I open my window as far as it will go and let the wind hit my face. It feels nice and refreshing. I thought it would keep me awake. But instead, the steady beat of the wind makes my eyes feel heavy, and I close them. Just as I'm about to fall off to sleep, I hear Auntie Heather say my name.

"What?" I ask tiredly.

She looks at me from the rearview mirror. "I was just saying that you know how you're the only girl?"

"Yes."

"Don't worry. Cerel also just turned twelve, and Hunter's thirteen now, so you'll have plenty in common and lots to do together. They play all the time with our neighbor's daughter back home. She's really good at soccer."

"Uh-huh. Thanks," I say back, not really thrilled by the idea. But I want to do my best to be polite, because I really like Auntie Heather. I close my eyes again and don't open them for a while. I fall asleep.

After what seems like just a minute, I wake up to my brother and Dominic yelling in my ear. "WAKE UP!" they both yell. I throw out my hand to shove Armand away, and he runs out of the car with Dominic. Sleepily, I get up and stumble around to the back of the car. I take my bags and walk through the gate to Auntie Heather's yard.

Auntie Heather approaches me and points to my bags. "Chloe, just let Hunter carry those in for you. He needs something to do." Behind her, Hunter comes down the porch steps. Gosh, he got tall, and he's only a year older than me? Does that mean I'm short for my age?

"I'm fine," I say to Auntie Heather. As soon as Hunter hears that, he spins around quickly and goes back into the house without a word. That's a bummer, because I've got this bruised foot and didn't really want to carry the bags up the stairs myself.

I walk up the porch steps and take off my shoes to enter the house. See, my Mom's from Asia, so she always wants us removing our shoes when we enter a home. When I take my first step inside, baby Sara runs up to me giggling. I smile down at her and kneel so that we can be face-to-face. Even kneeling, I'm still much higher than her. I poke her nose with my finger tip, and she giggles again and runs away. She hides behind a tall TV speaker, pokes her head out and just watches me. Babies kind of freak me out when they stare at me, especially when I'm in a restaurant and they do it over the back of their booth. I always want to look at their parents and ask, "Don't you see your kid? Why do you let him stick his face into other people's tables?"

"Chloe," Auntie Heather says. "Come with me. I have to show you your bedroom." I stand up and follow her through the kitchen and down into the basement. We walk by the washing machines, then into a thin hallway. It's not like a regular basement. It's really nice and sort of feels like a hotel.

There's a big bedroom at the end of the hallway with one bed near the entrance, a king-sized mattress on the floor and another bed opposite those and against a wall. My parents are standing by the back door of the room that leads to the outdoors. I want to see what's there, so I walk out and find myself on a wooden layer of floor that's made like a deck.

A warm breeze hits my face. Moving to the left, I walk up the stairs and into the back yard. It's a nice one. The boys have turned what looks like it used to be a lawn into a soccer field, and there are small, pretty rose bushes on the sides surrounded by light green grass. I take one more glance at the yard, then go back down into the bedroom.

"So the bathroom is through that sliding door," Auntie Heather says to my parents as I walk in the room. "And it uses a motion sensor, so I recommend you keep the door closed. Because if any of you roll in your sleep, the lights will turn on." The bed closest to the entrance from the hallway looks comfortable, so I sit on the edge of it. I fall right off, sort of sliding sideways, and the mattress flips off and leans against me.

What the-?! I'm totally confused.

"Oh, I forgot to tell you," Auntie Heather says, clearly trying to hold back her laughter. "That bed's a little wobbly."

A little? I try to shove the mattress aside, but it won't budge. I don't have any power to get this thing away from me, because it's awkward and kind of heavy. My parents and Auntie Heather lift the mattress and position it back on the bed.

"You okay?" Mom asks.

"I'm fine," I say to her. They go upstairs to have some brunch and leave me here, sitting on the floor.

7

When I walk upstairs, everyone's wearing their swim suits.

"Oh there you are, Chloe," Auntie Heather says from behind me. I turn around to look at her. "We're going to the beach soon, so you should probably change into your bathing suit," she says to me. I nod and go back down the basement stairs. I grab my spandex shorts and track & field shirt and lock myself in the bathroom.

I don't actually have a bathing suit, because my parents can never find one that is "appropriate" for me. They have this thing about how a bathing suit can fit and what it has to cover before I can buy it. But almost nothing in the stores where humans shop fits their standards. So I substitute a pair of spandex shorts with a pink stripe on the sides and just wear any shirt with that. It works. Plus, I have to admit, I never get any of those embarrassing wedgy moments that regular bathing suits give me. Also, when these dry, I can walk around town in them, because I'm not half naked.

I take my pants and shirt off and replace them with the spandex shorts and my track & field shirt, then I run upstairs to catch up with everybody else.

When I get upstairs, I grab the sunblock that sits by my Mom and run outside with it. I sit at the picnic table and start rubbing the sunblock onto my left leg. Someone comes out of the house, so I look up. Oh, nothing important…just Cerel. He joins me at the table with his own tube of sunblock and starts putting really thick globs of the stuff on his arms.

"I can't believe I'm staying in your bedroom," I say to him.

He smirks. "Which bed did you get?"

I don't reply at first, because I'm distracted by a single area of his arm where he hasn't rubbed the cream in yet. It bugs me. He clearly finished applying cream there and doesn't plan to go back. I want to reach over and wipe some over that area.

"Whatever. Don't answer me," he says.

"Huh? Oh. I was going to choose the bed by the TV, but, stupidly, I chose the broken one near the hallway. It almost killed me."

He laughs. "That's Faegan's bed, cuz he's the only one who can stay on it."

"How does he do it? It's like a balance beam."

Now he's rubbing cream between his nose and eyes. It's freaking me out, because blotches of cream seem to just miss his eyeball each time he swipes his face. But he's so casual about it. "I don't know, he's strange," he says as he adjusts his swim shirt.

What I like about Auntie Heather's family is that she tells her kids to wear special sun-blocking shirts as the tops of their bathing suits. The boys all wear them. It makes me feel much more relaxed, because I hate it when boys go around shirtless everywhere -- especially the ones who think they're such hunks. Gosh, it can be so gross sometimes.

Auntie Heather comes out of the house carrying baby Sara. "Okay. Cerel, can you go inside and get Hunter and tell him that you two can start biking to the beach now?" Cerel runs inside to get his brother. Auntie Heather manages to get Faegan, Armand, and Dominic into the car. Then she, Dad, Mom and I join them. She hands baby Sara to Faegan and tells him to hold onto her tightly. I don't get it. He's going to hold her? Where's her baby car seat?

"Okay," Auntie Heather says. "I think we can go now." She starts the engine, and we leave their house.

The car is super stuffy. At the beach I get out first, desperate for some air…and I'm trying to get away from Armand. Throughout the entire car ride, he and Dominic kept on singing this song called *Everything is Awesome.* That song is so annoying.

Auntie Heather and my parents come out of the car and open up the back lift gate. "Chloe?" Mom asks, "Can you carry some chairs for us?"

"Huh? Uh-sh-mmm," I say. This is another thing that happens when I wake up at three in the morning. I lose my ability to form normal words when I want to object. It's no problem getting two chairs out of the car, but they're heavier than they look, so I'll have to drag them all the way to the beach or whine to Dad for help. Then, Mom hands me her big green bag with clothes and a bunch of stuff in it – way too much stuff. "Really?" I ask her.

"Stop complaining, Chloe. I swear you need a therapist sometimes," Mom says.

"CEREL! HUNTER!" Auntie Heather yells and waves her arms over her head. Ow. My ears ring, as I take a few steps away from her and stand next to my dad. In the distance, I can see the two boys walking toward us from the bike rack area.

CITRA TENORE

"C'mon," Auntie Heather says to us. "They're going to take forever."

When we reach Cerel and Hunter, Auntie Heather hands them baby Sara like she's passing over a watermelon and then walks right past them.

My flip flops make so much noise, and the straps start to dig into my feet. We walk by a shaved ice stand, and already I start to feel my mouth water. But it's way too soon to ask for something to eat or drink. I already know Dad will say no. We shuffle down the super long and boiling hot sand-covered boardwalk that leads to the beach. The scraping noise against the sandy wood gives me the chills, like when someone scrapes their fingernails on a chalkboard. By the time we reach the end of the boardwalk, I see a large blue sign with bright red words, but they're just a blur to me. Probably important, but my eyeglasses are back at the house, and I'm way too tired to strain my brain to read the words. Everyone else is so distracted by the waves pounding the beach that they're looking way out and in the other direction from the sign. Oh well.

"Let's find a place that isn't very crowded," Dad says to everyone. But as he says that, Auntie Heather sets up the beach tent by a group of half-naked teenage girls. Gross. They look as unhappy as I do when we set up our umbrella and chairs next to them. Armand and Dominic are already wrestling in the sand and kicking it into the girls' faces as they try to sunbathe. Disaster.

While the adults set up all the beach stuff, I go down to the water with the five boys. Everyone jumps in, except for me, because of one flaw I see with this place. It's dangerous. I watch people go in the water, but as soon as they do, large waves push them to shore like pieces of paper in a windstorm and then rip them back into the ocean. The waves are so huge, and I'm guessing this is probably the reason why this beach is called Surfside Beach.

Behind me, Mom runs into the water without a single concern. Creepy. I'm not sure why it's creepy to me when Mom does that kind of thing, but it is. It's as if I'm used to seeing her cook and sit and knit, not go berserk in nature. "C'mon,

Chloe!" Armand yells as a large wave pushes him toward me. "It's so fun! Why aren't you coming in?" Swoosh! He washes up onto shore like a dead fish.

"Uhh, maybe it's the fact that you were twenty feet from me when you started that sentence and now you're only two feet away," I say. He scrunches up his face at me as if he smelled some old broccoli or something. I start to turn around to gaze far down the beach, when all of a sudden I'm grabbed by the lower back and flipped upside down like a piece of raw pizza dough. I'm completely helpless and hanging with a view of the beach over the sky. I may barf. All I can do is turn my head and see my dad laughing. Oh crud…here we go. I can feel him getting ready to toss me. But I dig deep and start fighting back by thrashing my arms and legs.

"No!" I yell. Hunter and Cerel come out of the water laughing and help my dad by grabbing my feet. I try to wiggle them, but it's no use. "Stop!" But they quickly toss me into the water, and salty guck flows into my gaping mouth. I lift my head out of the water and look for my dad. But just as I'm about to run after him…bam! A huge wave blasts me from behind, knocks me over and pushes me into the feet of Armand and Cerel. Gross. I spit a bunch of sand out of my mouth, which I make sure "accidently" lands on Cerel's leg.

"Never be unaware at the beach," my dad says while looking down at me. I just let my head fall onto the sand and my entire body go limp. But that's not a good idea, because the ocean current jerks me into the water, and then another wave pushes me back to Cerel's feet. He crosses his arms and looks down at me like he's a mighty warrior who just defeated me. I grab his feet and drag him into the water. Ha. Revenge! Unfortunately, I'm still laying down on the ground, so I get pulled back into the water by another wave. I give up. I have to laugh along with everyone else, because it actually is pretty funny being tossed around like some little rubber duck in a waterfall.

"GET DOMINIC!" my dad screams. We all get up and run after Dominic. I grab his legs, Cerel and Hunter get him by the arms, and my dad carries his body. "ONE! TWO! THREE!" Dad yells, and we throw Dominic. He flies into the water, and for a few seconds he doesn't come up. Suddenly, he appears at my feet from out of nowhere. "Bye-bye," he says in a little, evil baby voice. He grabs my feet, and I fall onto the sand. Then another large wave comes up from behind me, and I go under...again. When I come back up, everyone's laughing at me.

I run after Dominic and grab him. I try to pick him up but my weak and lame body is just way too, well...weak and lame. Winning this little "I-throw-you, you-throw-me" game is very important to me. I mean, I know it's a stupid little thing, but seriously, I will not lose to an eight-year-old boy! As Dominic starts doing some weird dance move that involves splashing me, I splash him back. Then I lightly kick him behind the left knee, and he falls into the water. Mean, I know. Mom yells my name and gives me a really dirty look for using such a cheap move to beat up a little kid. "Sorry!" I yell to Dominic.

I try to act all innocent for a minute and pretend I don't mean to, but dump Cerel. He gets up and pushes me into the water, and the current pulls me back yet again. I stand up before the next wave can take me and I leap toward him. But as I do, Hunter and my dad come to his defense and throw me in again. Really, Dad? Five boys against one girl, and you help defend them? "You guys are lame," I say. "Not one of you can beat a dainty girl like me by yourself."

"Okay, then," Dad says. He runs toward me, grabs me again, and throws me into the water. I stay under long enough to swipe Cerel's left foot and Hunter's right. They wobble and fall face first. As their heads appear, a huge wave slams into them, and they both come up choking on mouthfuls of salt water. I laugh. I laugh out loud at their weakness. I'm starting to like this beach.

"Guys!" we all turn around, and Auntie Heather is standing by the water. "Come out for a few minutes to have some lunch."

I bite into my Brie cheese sandwich while smacking a wasp away. But my hand brushes the sand, which gets all over my food. "Stupid beach sand," I say out loud. I love Brie cheese, and who knows when I'll find a sandwich like that again.

Armand and Dominic look at me and start saying, "Ooo, she said stupid. She said stupid."

"You guys are so childish," I tell them. Like they care.

I wipe my hands against my shorts, then I put my food on Dad's plate, which makes him groan. "Fine," he says to me. "But don't just waste food. There are people all over the world who can't afford-"

"I know," I say, while standing up and heading to the water to wash my hands.

As I dunk my hands in the ocean, something slimy moves across the top of my bruised toe, the one I hurt when I kicked my bed last night. I

* 81 *

wonder what that could…"AH!!" I shout. On my foot is a big (but tiny), flesh eating (maybe not flesh eating)…crab. Ew. I kick my foot up, and the crab goes flying back into the water. I turn around to run and tell Dad, but all five boys and baby Sara are coming up behind me.

"What happened to you?" Dominic asks me like I'm nuts.

"You ask too many questions," I answer.

Then Cerel turns to Dominic. "Yeah, why do you ask so many questions?" Then he turns to me. "So, what happened to you?"

"Come here and take a look at this creepy little crab," I say. Just as Dominic and Cerel bend over to investigate, I push them from behind, and into the waves they go.

We spend the next couple of hours dumping each other in the waves. I'm so exhausted by the constant slamming and spinning that I barely have enough energy to walk to the car when we leave.

8

"I think that Lady Gaga is much worse," Cerel says to me. Hunter nods and goes back to reading his book. We sit at the picnic table in front of their house talking about who's crazier, Kesha or Lady Gaga.

I shake my head. "No, I think they're equally crazy."

"Why are we even talking about this in the first place?" Hunter asks us. "And by the way, she isn't nearly as bad as-"

"Chloe," I turn around and once again, Auntie Heather is standing right next to me. How does she sneak up without me ever hearing it?

"Oh...uh…hi," I say to her.

"So," she says. "I have your towels and stuff like that." She leans a bit closer to me and whispers, even though I know that the two boys can hear her. "Your mother told me that you hit that stage and you already had your first you-know-what. So I thought that you should be the first kid to shower, with all the beach sand and everything." She hands me the towel. "Shower's just around the back. If you have any...secret items...you can put them in this little bag." She hands me a clear plastic bag and walks back into the house.

I kind of just stare at her for a moment, not really knowing what to say. Seriously? I can't believe she just said that...here! I can feel the heat and embarrassment on my face, like I'm on fire and have a big blazing "loser" etched across my forehead.

"Auntie Heather!" I yell to her. "Where's the shower?"

She peeks her head out through the door. "It's in the back yard by the boys' soccer net."

It's what?! Who puts a shower next to a soccer net? I can't believe it's outside. I turn around and face Cerel and Hunter.

"Well that's a fun fact to know about you," Cerel says laughing. I give him a glare and then try to look the other way. That just makes the two of them laugh.

Why would she say something like that? I feel my cheeks growing hot as I look from Hunter to Cerel, then Cerel back to Hunter. "Shower's that way," Cerel says while pointing to the backyard. I nod and leave the table, totally mortified.

OK. I'm completely naked outdoors in a yard surrounded by boys playing soccer. And this isn't just some weird dream. It's actually happening.

Alright, so technically there are four walls around me, but they're made of that wood from a picket fence and don't reach all the way to the floor. It creeps me out. Like those bathroom stalls at school. Who can actually go number two on a toilet that doesn't have full privacy? Not me, unless I'm totally having stomach issues and it just won't stop. Anyway, the point is, one of them could easily poke his head under the shower wall and see me. Not to mention, every sound outside the wall seems to be happening in here. They're so close.

Armand yells for a pass, and I jump, because it sounds like he's standing next to me. So, I stuff all my dirty clothes around the edges of the floor where they meet the wall. This mostly blocks the space, but it still sounds like everything is wide open. Well, I can't think of any better way to hide, and now the water's starting to warm up, so I may as well try to go with the flow. What choice do I have?

The hot water hits my back and actually feels refreshing. Wow, this shower is much better than I thought it would be. That is, until the soccer ball rolls up close and a boy comes to get it. I don't know who it is, and he's not saying anything, but I can sense his presence. "I know you're there," I say, trying to sound all confident. But then I hear nothing. Did he leave while I was talking? Is he being creepy and staying near? I wait a minute, and it seems like forever. For some reason I'm holding my breath.

Finally, I think he had to have left, because what fun would there be in standing silent outside a shower? I reach for the shampoo bottle and put some on my head. I scrub through all my hair, and when I hold my hand in front of my face, I see a bunch of sand crystals. Looking down, they're all over the tops of my feet now. Yuck. Beach-going really is a dirty hobby.

Out of nowhere, a big hornet lands on my nose, and I fall to the ground swiping my face in fear. But then I quickly jump up, paranoid that someone will peek through the shower at ground level. As I scramble to my feet, the water splashes the soap that's on my bangs right into my eyes. "IT BURNS!" I scream. It feels like the soap is drilling holes into my eyes and filling them with red hot lava. I stumble into the door, which flies open.

I yelp and quickly pull the door shut. Voices come closer from the other side of the shower, and I try locking the door. There's no lock! I didn't know there was NO LOCK on the door! How ridiculous is that? You can't send a girl into the middle of a field and into a shower that has no lock. I mean, wait a minute...If there's no lock, then that means anyone could come in right now and see me stumbling around blind and naked. I better get the soap out of my eyes before I accidentally trip into the middle of their soccer game.

After rinsing all the soap out, I turn off the shower and quickly reach for my towel. It's not there. I forgot my towel. Oh God. How did I forget my towel? Could this get any worse? Apparently, it can. Because now I have to ask the voices that are five feet away to bring me a towel.

"Anyone there?" I ask. I hear footsteps approach, and the voices all come to a sudden hush.

"Yeah, I'm here," Someone says. I can tell that it's Dominic. On the bright side, at least it isn't one of the boys my age, because that would be much worse.

"Umm…Dominic? Can you bring me a towel?" I ask. I can feel my heart beating against my chest.

"Sure," he answers through the wall. I hear him walk in the other direction. "She wants me to get her a towel," he says to someone. Great. I can't wait for this story to get out.

I hit a mosquito away that's zoning in on my leg. Looking around the floor with my clothes spread along the sides, I see a big pile of the adults' clothes in the corner to my right. Auntie Heather told everyone to pile their clothes in a corner so that she could clean them all together. Gross. I don't want to see dirty adult clothing, and I don't want to go near them. The problem is, my bra is sitting on the top of the pile for everyone to see. I didn't think about that. I want so badly to put that bra under my shirt, but there's a big black spider sitting in a web right over the pile where the bra is. I am not a fan of outdoor showers – just too many bugs. I start to shiver. Even though it's hot today, my pores are now open. I hope Dominic gets back soon with that towel.

"Chloe?" I hear Dominic say. "I have your towel." Phew, great timing.

"Oh, thanks. Just throw it over." He throws the towel over the wall to my left, and it lands on my head.

I dry myself, wrap the towel around my body, then open the door and put on my flip flops. The towel is way too small. Good thing it's not a long walk to my room. I scoot down the stairs behind the boys' soccer game and reach for the door handle to the bedroom. I try to open the door, but it's locked. I jiggle the handle hard, and through the window I see that Armand and Dominic are actually laughing and pointing at me from the other side of the door. They must have run down here to lock me out.

"You open that door right now, you little dweebs!" I yell. But they just run away from the window and start waving their butts at me from the middle of the room. Idiots.

So now I have two choices. I could go through the boys' soccer game and around the house to the front door, passing the picnic table where Hunter and Cerel are reading. Or, I can sneak around the other side of the house and into the kitchen entrance. Kitchen it is, because I'm not daring to go past those two while wearing just a tiny towel.

I scamper quietly up the stairs and take a left, rushing by the side of the house that faces the neighbors' home. As I do, I hear a noise off to my right. Already, I feel some sweat trickling down the back of my neck. I turn to see a man and woman grilling food. They stop grilling and look over at me. I pull my towel up higher, attempting to cover myself to the neck. I sort of let out a sound that's a cross between a whimper and a shriek, then run into the kitchen entrance of the house and slam the door behind me.

Just as I think I'm in the clear, Hunter and Auntie Heather appear right in front of me. They stop short, just five feet away, and look at me like I'm naked. This is a nightmare. I run down the basement steps, past the laundry and into our

guest bedroom. Armand and Dominic are gone.
I'll get them for this.

9

I go over to the rack holding my bags and take out my clothes. I'm done being on display, so I get dressed in the bathroom, the only safe place with a locking door. After dressing, I reach into my bag and pull out City of Bones. Seriously, whoever designed this front cover is nuts. I sneak out the back door, see that the picnic table is empty, and quietly settle down there to read. Finally, some peace and quiet. Just me and my new book.

After a couple minutes, Hunter and Cerel come out holding books and plop themselves down at the table across from me. Cerel's book has a really weird cover. It's a picture of what looks like a mouse jumping through a light bulb. I try to ignore them and bury my head into my book.

"How was your shower?" Cerel asks from behind his book, not looking up at me.

"Fine," I reply tersely and don't look up.

"That's not what I heard," he argues. "And your walk back…towel girl?"

"Shuddup."

"Well, you're supposed to get dressed instead of running around everywhere in a towel," says Hunter.

"Is there a point to this?" I ask. "Did I damage anyone? No."

Silence. I can almost feel Cerel searching his brain for a sarcastic comment, but nothing comes out of his mouth except a little push of air. A long hush falls over the table. After a few minutes, Hunter interrupts my reading. "What is that?" he asks. I look up, and he gestures to the front cover of my book.

"It's a book." I'm obviously not in the mood.

"Oh I read that!" Cerel says. "It's garbage."

"Cerel, maybe she likes it. Do you?" Hunter asks me.

"Oh no. My friend Adiva liked it and so I'm just-"

But I get cut off by my brother running towards us wearing just a towel around his waist and yelling, "Chloe! Chloeeeeeeee!"

"I hear you!" I bark at him.

"Chloe! I was in the shower!" He looks around at everyone at the table. "I was in the shower."

"Good for you," I say.

"So, I was in the shower…"

"I know! Just get on with it! You always start your stories like seven times."

"OK, so I was in the shower, and you know how we're supposed to put our clothes in the corner?"

Oh no. Don't say it. Please, Armand, don't you dare.

He dares. "I-I SAW YOUR BRA!"

And here we go again.

"Yah, your bra! It's right there in the corner. Go look, guys!" He starts jumping up and down and pointing with one hand toward the direction of the outdoor shower while his other hand holds his towel from falling off his waist. Hunter and Cerel crack up. Cerel drops his book, falls to the ground and rolls around holding his stomach while he laughs hysterically. He gets going so much, it looks like he can't breathe. Hunter laughs so hard that he starts snorting.

"D-d-did you h-hear your brother s-say that?" Cerel struggles to ask while consumed with laughter. Dominic and Armand run back toward the shower.

I will get Armand for this. Now I owe him double, but not yet. I'd only make things worse by reacting in front of the other boys.

When he finally gains control of himself, Cerel sits back at the table. I look under it, spot his legs and kick them. But he doesn't fall in pain like I wish he would. He just laughs even harder. After he and Hunter finish giggling and smiling at me, we all just stare at each other for a few seconds.

"Soooo, do either of you like Ariana Grande?" I ask them, obviously trying to change the subject.

Hunter plays along. "No."

"Oh, man!" Cerel says. "I love her. How can you not love the song Problem? So great."

I smile. At least I managed to move onto another subject. "It's okay I guess."

"Yeah," Cerel says. "Also she is HOT! I mean, like, there are some really pretty girls and stuff, but she is HOT!"

"Yeah, yeah, we get it," I say to him. "And by the way, you do know she's twenty-one and your only twelve, right?"

"Whatever. She is so h-"

"What's gotten into you?" Hunter asks, looking at Cerel with one eyebrow raised.

"Yeah you weirdo," I agree. He just sits there happily.

"Anyway," I say. "Did you see the movie…City of Bones?"

"Yeah," Cerel says. "It was terrible. And the story stinks. There's absolutely no point to it."

"Yes there was-" I start to disagree, but once again, get interrupted. Seems to be happening a lot today.

"Hey guys!" We all turn around, and to my surprise, it isn't Auntie Heather or Armand or Dominic with something to embarrass me. It's Uncle Brygus.

"Hi," I say to him, "Umm…my dad's inside."

"Thanks," he says and goes into the house.

"So did you like the movie?" Cerel asks me.

"It was alright."

The three of us stop talking and just awkwardly exchange glances for a minute. We don't really know what to say to each other all the time, because we're not like school friends who see each other every day. But we do see each other sometimes, so we're more than just strangers. We're definitely not 'framily' but not just acquaintances either. It's weird. Eventually, Cerel brakes the silence.

"Did you hear about the mattress falling on Chloe this morning?" he asks Hunter. Hunter looks at me amusedly. I groan.

"Lemme guess," Hunter says. "You chose Faegan's bed."

I nod. "I wasn't expecting it. Seriously, couldn't your mom have warned me before I sat on it?"

Cerel looks at us blankly. "I need to shower. My armpits stink," he says. Well that definitely wasn't the answer I was expecting. Ew. He walks away, and I open up my book again.

"I didn't even know he read that," Hunter says whispering to himself and looking at my book. "How did I not see it?"

"Who knows," I say, trying to drift into my story. But Armand and Dominic come running out of the house holding two plastic baseball bats and no ball. Oh no. I know what this means. Whenever Armand's got one of those things, it's his chance to smack me. And if he gets caught, he always says something like I was trying to break it or steal it from him. Unfortunately, I can't really defend myself with just a book.

10

I hold the icepack to my right knee and scrunch up my face as Cerel and Hunter look on. Armand and Dominic never meant to hurt me. They just wanted to scare me by swinging the bats around my body. But Armand ended up banging my right knee and my left arm, which already has a bruise on it. What gets me is they're not even grounded or in trouble because "they're on vacation." Like that should matter. So what? They get to run around the back yard and hurt people? But I have to sit in front of Hunter and Cerel who keep laughing at me.

"It's not funny," I tell the two of them.

Cerel's face turns all red as he struggles to hold in his laughter. "Yeah it is," he says. "You should've seen your face. You were all, like, 'Oh my God, I'm gonna die!' It was hilarious!"

"Oh please," I mutter.

"You've got to admit," Hunter perks up. "It was pretty funny the way you panicked."

"I guess. If you're an immature…"

I don't have the energy to come up with some line that will burn them. Plus, my bruises are bugging me. Auntie Heather comes out of the house and stands over the three of us with her hands on her hips. "So," she says. "We're going next door in a few minutes for dinner with the neighbors. Which means, you guys need to get ready." She walks away and we sit there.

NO. I can't go to the neighbors' house. They just saw me running around outside half naked, wearing just a towel. What am I going to do? I want to disappear. I wish I had a ton of makeup. I'd disguise myself as someone else. The neighbors will definitely remember my face, because they stared at me for what felt like a full minute.

"What's wrong with you?" Hunter asks me. "You're turning all red and stuff."

"Umm, I don't know," I lie.

"Are you always this way when you have to meet new people?" he asks.

"Idiots. That's what I'm afraid of, and I'm surrounded by them," I say.

Cerel puts up his hands as if he were surrendering to the police. "What did I do?" he asks. I just roll my eyes, and he grunts. Whatever, I hope the food is good.

I follow my dad to the neighbors' house. Apparently, they moved to Massachusetts from the Philippines last year. That makes my mom happy, because she's Indonesian and is excited whenever she gets the chance to meet other people from Southeast Asia and try their food. All those countries – Indonesia, Malaysia, Vietnam, and Cambodia – they all serve spicy dishes. Mom says she's craving spicy food, as if she doesn't have it all the time.

As for me, I'm genetically more like my dad. He grew up here and is 100 percent Italian-American. Well, he has a little French and Canadian sprinkled in, too, but everybody says that. My brother is more like my mom than my dad. He has darker skin and loves eating fishy food. I can't stand fish unless it's something like salmon or shrimp. I'm more of a bread-and-cheese type of person.

In front of me, Dad and the others stop at the backyard of the neighbors' house, causing me to bump into Faegan's back. "Sorry," I whisper. He just smiles and moves on. Faegan's not really like his brothers. He's pretty calm and peaceful…not always looking to show off or burn somebody. The bruise on my right arm is now purple, the one on my foot is throbbing, and the spot on my right knee where Armand hit is now itchy and painful. It looks disgusting.

A little girl runs up to us with a basket of bread and hands us each a piece. "Thank you," we say.

She smiles and gives a nod. We all walk to the back deck by the house. A man and lady stand over a huge grill cooking tons of meat. I recognize them from my half-naked towel episode and quickly put my head down so they don't notice me. I try squeezing between Faegan's shoulder and the side of the house, but he puts this weird look on his face and slides away from me. My parents follow Auntie Heather and Uncle Brygus up the deck steps so that they can introduce us kids to the grilling adults. Great. The last thing I wanted was to be formally introduced. It would be like, "Hi, so you shower outdoors and run around with no clothes on, huh? That's nice."

I keep my head down, but Dad nudges me. "Put your head up. You're not two," he whispers. Wow, that makes me feel much better. Now I have to look these people in the eye, shake their hands, smile, and act all happy to be here.

"Nice to meet you," I say to the couple when I reach the top of the steps. I put my hand out to shake theirs. They stare at me for a second, as if they recognize me (they probably do), then they both shake my hand. But they don't really speak. They just give me big smiles and say "Hi. You eat. You eat."

Oh yeah, they definitely just moved here from the Philippines. I've seen this before with some of Mom's Indonesian relatives. People who just move here always tell me to eat. It's like it gives us all something to do when we don't know how to speak enough of each other's language to have a real conversation. I thank them, pick up a plate and head down the deck stairs to their picnic table that's full of food.

I look at the food and think that it looks…well…interesting. I'm dying for a burger and fries. I always feel that way after a day at the beach. Dad says it's because I crave salt after sweating it all away. But this is Southeast Asian food, so no fries or burgers. It's all rice, veggies and meat dishes in sauces. I can't tell if they're fish, beef, pork or chicken because the sauces are all darkly colored. Actually, the sauces might not be so dark. It's just that there's only one light on the entire yard, so everything appears dark.

I figure soup will be safest, because I like the Indonesian soup that my mom's friends make. I take a bowl and put some soup into it, then swipe a few crackers. As soon as the hot broth hits the back of my throat, I gag. Two weird sounds come out...kind of like eck-ksterck, and I have to stop myself from throwing up. Wow that's spicy! Thank God I took those acting classes this summer, because a couple people turned to me when they heard the noise. I put on my happiest face and pointed my spoon at the soup bowl. "Sorry, eating too fast. You have to try this soup."

My mother starts beaming with delight. She puts her hand on the other Asian lady's arm and says, "I'm really trying to get them to appreciate our culture. It's so good for them to eat our food. It's much more unique." Unique. Yes, I have to agree with her. Reluctantly, I swallow the unique liquid and stuff my mouth with crackers to absorb the spice.

"You like it?" the Filipino woman asks, while peeking to see if my bowl is empty. I look back at her with a smile, doing my best to hide the fact that my throat's burning up.

"Mm, it's really different," I reply. "It's nothing like boring American food." The perfect answer. She seems satisfied, and I didn't have to admit that the spice is killing me.

"So happy you like," she says. And with that, she walks away.

Phew! It worked. I look at my brother and Dominic as they try the soup and almost gag themselves. I guess they fell for my act, too. Hah! Revenge through acting! Then, I race over to the drink cooler, grab some ice cubes and stuff them in my mouth. They melt away almost instantly. Armand and Dominic scream and follow right behind me. But instead of grabbing a few cubes, they dunk their heads into the cooler and bob for ice.

"Why are you wearing sneakers?" I turn around to see Cerel standing there holding Sara by the hand.

"Umm, I like to keep my feet clean," I say. "And they're very comfortable."

He looks dumbfounded, as if I just told him Santa is real. "But you're on vacation," he says.

"So…?"

"So, don't you ever take your shoes and socks off when you're at the beach?"

Now it's my turn to look at him in stunned surprise. "Of course I take my shoes and socks off at the beach, but I like the feeling of shoes. Why are we even discussing this?"

"I dunno," he says. He walks away with Sara, as she holds onto him with one hand and a stuffed animal tucked under her arm. She's so adorable. Adorable and happy.

11

"So, you guys are separated by a wall from the boys' bedroom," Auntie Heather tells us. She points to the door by my bed. "That door lets you go into their room, and they can come into here because there's no lock. I'm going to leave it open so it doesn't get too stuffy while everyone sleeps."

Did I hear that the wrong way? She's leaving the door to the boys' room open, and I'm right next to it. Great, now they can hear me tossing and turning and snoring. And I know boys. There will be tons of weird noises and gross things coming out of their room during the night. Just what every girl wants.

I get my toothbrush and go into the bathroom. The light turns on automatically, and I brush my teeth. That's cool. When I'm done, I spit the gross gunk out of my mouth and rinse with water. I'm about to get into bed when Faegan walks by and looks at me.

"Why are you wearing socks to bed?" he asks.

I roll my eyes. "Seriously?! What do you guys have against shoes and socks?" I get under the covers.

He looks surprised by my reaction. "Geez, sorry," he says as he puts his head down and shuffles out of the room as fast as possible.

My dad turns off all the lights and slides the bathroom door closed. That way, the motion-sensing lights won't turn on if one of us rolls in our sleep or something. The rest of the boys go through the door by my bed, and I look around at my family. Armand is about to sleep on the couch. My parents settle into the mattress on the floor, and I lay on this contraption that only looks like a bed. It's more like a mattress on a long, metal swivel stick...like some kind of amusement park ride – "First person to stay on the thingy for 30 seconds wins a prize!"

Whatever. It's been a super long day. I plop my head down and fall asleep.

I can feel the hardened rock thing. It seems to be right at the edge of my nostril, just barely inside. What time is it? Darkness surrounds me, as well as the whirring sound of the fan that's on the bedside table. I guess it's like two in the morning, because everything else is dead quiet. This hard booger is keeping me awake. Once I know one's there, especially so close to coming out, I have to get it immediately. Otherwise, I won't be able to go back to sleep.

I remember Mom put a tissue box on the table earlier, so I blindly reach for it, tapping my hand around the top of the table. It's not there. I know I saw it earlier. How frustrating. Someone must have moved it. Dad's the closest to me, so I whisper to him. "Dad. Dad." I hear him groan, but he doesn't wake up. I try a little louder. "Dad!"

"What?" he asks, clearly annoyed to be awakened.

"Have you seen the tissue box?"

He grunts, then answers, "Under the bedside table."

"I looked there."

"Look harder," he says. Well that helps, doesn't it?

I can partially reach the underside of the table, but feel no tissue box there. I'll have to reach further underneath to find it. So, I roll over to my left to face the table and stretch my arm forward. As I do, there's a weird sound of scraping metal and then…'Boing!' Suddenly, I'm flipping off the bed toward the table.

In the pitch black night, everything seems to happen in slow motion, and it seems like ten full seconds before my flight ends. I land hard, and the mattress comes down, too. I swing my arm fast to protect my head, but my arm nails the leg of the table. "Ow!" I yell. Suddenly, the fan comes down spinning right by my head, and without warning, grabs my hair.

"HELP!" I yell. The place quickly turns into a madhouse, and I can hear my mother gasping through my yells and Dad's commands.

"Turn the lights on!" I hear Dominic and Cerel say. How'd they get here so fast?! Ouch, my hair! It feels like the fan is eating it all up. "Ouch! Help me!" I shriek. I can't be sure, but it feels like half my hair is snagged and getting twisted in the blades. I thrash my arms and legs around and yell for Dad to help.

"Her hair is stuck. The fan!" Oh great. That's Hunter's voice. What's next? Channel 7 news? Auntie Heather and Uncle Brygus run into the room. This kills! I just wanted a tissue!

My body is now stuck to the floor, thanks to the mattress on my back. I feel the weight getting lifted off me, and then the entire mattress is tossed to the side. I'd stand up right now, but this stupid fan is chomping my hair and won't let go. Finally, somebody turns the lights on, and Dad unplugs the fan.

"Cerel, grab the scissors from the bathroom counter," Auntie Heather orders. Why does she want scissors?! No! She's going to cut my hair! My beautiful, luscious hair! No time goes by when Cerel comes running towards me with a sharp pair of scissors, laughing and looking like some crazed lunatic murderer. For a second, I'm afraid that HE is the one who is going to cut my hair. NO, NO! Instead, he hands the scissors to his dad, who comes right towards my head quickly.

"Have you ever done this before?!" I shout.

"Uhh, no. But I doubt anybody else here has either," he responds calmly.

I can't see him, but I can tell that he doesn't know how to do this. "Why don't you just turn the fan on again, but backwards?" I ask.

"No such thing," he says. "Relax. This won't hurt a bit."

I try to argue, but I'm face-down in the carpet and have no control over the situation. Still, I get a few words out. "I'm not worried about that. I'm trying to grow my-"

Too late. He has already cut the entangled hair from my head. I do nothing but shriek.

12

Cerel bites into his toast. "You're such a girl," he says to me as he chews.

I roll my eyes. "Well, that would make a lot of sense since I was born female."

"No. I mean, you're complaining about your hair looking bad, because one side is two inches too short while the other is perfect," he says while over-dramatically pretending to flip long hair off his shoulders.

"Okay, so what do you think I should do about my hair?"

"How am I supposed to know? I'm not a girl."

"Are you saying I should just chop the rest of it? Because that's pretty much what your dad did last night. He just chopped it right off. I mean, he's a doctor, for God's sake. I thought he'd have a little more talent with a pair of scissors."

"Yeah, that was funny," says Hunter, turning the page of his book without looking up. "Still, he's not a surgeon. He's just a regular doctor."

"CHLOE!" Armand yells in excitement and comes near us. "We're going to the beach!"

"Can't I get my hair done first? I don't want to go anywhere in public looking like this."

"Yeah, Mom says she wants you on the back deck so she can cut your hair."

"Thank you," I say and walk past him.

Mom is talking to Auntie Heather in front of a chair on the back deck. I sit in the chair and feel her hairbrush instantly grab my hair. Then there are some little snip-snips as she trims it. "Okay!" she says gleefully. "We're done!" Auntie Heather hands me a mirror and smiles.

Well, this is different. I actually like it. The ends don't look chopped like the way Mom usually cuts them. They're actually kind of spikey. Very funky and unusual. "Thanks," I say. I leave and quickly get changed into my beach clothes. Maybe this weekend won't be a total loss.

I walk down the path to the beach. Since I have my book and Mom's reading glasses, I may as well read that extra-large sign that stands near the end of the boardwalk. The only problem is that, after I read it, I don't want to remember what I just read. It says in big bold letters, Caution: Sharks and Jellyfish in These Waters.

Wow.

"I just read that sign," I tell my dad as we exit the boardwalk toward the water. "I'm staying on the blanket and reading my book."

He laughs and starts trudging through the sand and onto the beach. "They just put those there so they don't get sued," he says. "It's state law. There are no sharks or jellies here, and Uncle Brygus says there's never been any seen around Nantucket. There are millions of those signs on

Mass beaches. They're all over the place when we go to the beach in Ipswich. Remember?"

I don't remember, but I have to admit that I've never been too aware of stuff like that before this year. Anyway, that's a relief to know.

Armand and Dominic carry their boogie boards and talk about Minecraft. We set up our beach umbrella at an empty spot with no one anywhere near us. Phew. Yesterday, it was pretty uncomfortable with those string bikini girls in our faces. I grab one of the boogie boards from Armand and Dominic and run into the water. Actually, I limp into the water. My bruised foot and cut knee both still hurt a lot. I figure floating around on the board will feel much better than fighting in the waves with the boys today.

"Ow!" I exclaim. People look over to me from all directions, and I quickly stand up, trying not to grab too much attention. I look down and find a sharp rock sticking out of the sand. So that's what I tripped on. There's a huge scrape on the bottom of my left foot. It might not be oozing with blood, but it definitely hurts. I rub my foot gently, because I don't want to open the scrape.

I continue limping back into the water. I steady myself onto the boogie board and start paddling. After a few minutes of this, I stop paddling and just float. In the distance, I can hear the sound of seagulls and kids playing. It's funny how kids yelling and playing sounds nice from far away, but terrible up close.

I float a little longer, until for some reason, I feel my left leg getting warm. The rest of my body is kind of cold from the water and the clouds covering the sun, but my leg feels strange. As if some type of warm liquid were spreading over it. I ignore the feeling for a while and just sit there….until I start getting really annoyed. I struggle to get up from my comfortable position, look down my leg and gasp.

I panic and freeze. But then, I realize it doesn't help anyone to just sit in the middle of the ocean, trying not to scream. The scrape on my foot must have opened, and now I'm bleeding. Great. I'm pretty far from shore. I don't feel any pain, but the sight of the blood spilling out makes me feel nauseous. I look back to the beach and scan the crowd for my dad. Only, I don't want the others to come because they'll make a huge deal about it. I finally find a group splashing and throwing each other into the water. Yup, that's them.

I awkwardly paddle toward shore. "Dad!" I yell, but he's too busy trying not to get tackled by Cerel and Armand. Figures. I've never really been the type that screams a lot, which is why the teachers at school are always like "speak up sweetie" whenever I read something out loud. "Sweetie". I don't like it when teachers say that. It's weird for some reason.

"Dad!" I scream now. Unfortunately, it isn't him who hears me. It's Armand, Cerel, and Dominic…just what I wanted. But their approach seems to catch Dad's eye.

"Dad!" Third time's a charm. He finally hears me. "Can you come over here…ALONE?"

He says something to the boys, and they reluctantly stop chasing me, but hover to see what's happening. I paddle a little to get closer to Dad and stop when I reach him.

"What's going on?" he asks, but pauses when he sees the blood. "Geez Chloe, Do you have a cut on you?"

I lift up my foot, which now looks like someone took some red paint and covered my skin with it.

"I tripped on a rock."

"You tripped on a rock?"

"Okay so I was running to the shore with the boogie board, but I wasn't watching where I was going and stepped on this sharp rock thing sticking out of the sand. But that's not the point-"

He doesn't listen, "-Chloe, I've told you so many times, you have to watch where you're going wherever you are." He pauses, then says, "Now, we have to get you out of the ocean because of the sharks."

"The sharks?! But you told me there were no sharks!"

"Yes, I told you that because I didn't want you to get all paranoid about the sharks and just sit on the blanket doing nothing."

"Okay, so can we get out of here?"

"Sure, but you need to get to the first aid station, unless Auntie Heather brought some-"

"Why is her leg red?" Dad and I turn around to find Armand and Dominic only a few feet away and staring at us.

Dominic laughs and points at me. "Did you get a really bad sunburn?"

How does he think it's a sunburn? Sunburns are your skin, but blood is literally leaking (I know, gross) out of my foot. I ignore them, and Dad grabs the rope of the boogie board and drags me to the shore. When we finally reach the shallow water I jump off the boogie board. I run with a huge limp back to the beach umbrella, doing my best to not make some big scene.

"Hi Chloe," Auntie Heather says, not noticing my leg as she fixes Zara's hair. "Did you have fun in-"

Now she sees it. The blood is gathering in the sand around my foot.

"How did you-"

"Long story," Dad cuts her off from behind. "We need some type of first aid or a bandage. Do you have any?"

"Umm..." she wanders and searches through her bag.

Mom comes out from behind the umbrella. "Chloe, what happened to your foot?!"

"Tripped on a rock." I really don't feel like explaining right now. But everybody keeps asking the same question, "Chloe, how'd you get that big cut?" and "Why's it bleeding so much?"

"Sorry I don't have any bandages," says Auntie Heather, "But there's a first aid station just on the other side of the boardwalk. They'll fix it up fast."

Dad and I slip away and go to the first aid station. It's really just a small tent with a few boxes and two chairs, hardly anything big, but at least it's here. No one's inside, so I just sit on one of the chairs and wait while Dad runs over to the lifeguard and asks about the first aid.

I take one of the tissues from the table and press it against my cut since I don't want any more blood to leak out. The tissue gets all red and wet very fast, so I start using three at a time because the sight of blood just makes me want to vomit…especially when it's my own.

Dad finally comes back with a girl walking next to him. I say a girl, but she's probably around her twenties.

"Okay," she says joyfully as she grabs a first aid kit. "We're gonna- oh my."

I can't help myself but to laugh a little bit at her reaction, and I can't blame her because my entire lower leg is red like a tomato. It looks way worse than it is.

"How hard did you fall?" she asks while cleaning my leg with some type of wipe. The wipe stings a little when it brushes over the cut, probably has some type of disinfecting chemical in there.

"I fell on a sharp rock sticking out of the sand," I tell her, and she nods.

"Probably another dead crab. There are a ton of those cracked shells just lying around waiting for people to step on them. It's pretty dangerous. About twice a day I get people coming in here all bloodied by a piece of crab shell that cut them, and sometimes, the splinters can be really tough to remove."

I squirm a little in my seat, just imagining a crab shell going into my skin. EW, I'm kind of grossed out right now. This just proves that always wearing something on my feet is a good idea. I'll have to find a pair of those surfer sneakers. She keeps going on about why the clean-up crew should pick up the shells, and I nod occasionally but try not to listen to the details whenever she explains recent injuries. Something tells me that she gets kind of bored around here, just sitting in a tent all day and fixing people.

After she cleans my leg, she patches up the cut with a large bandage. "There you go, oh and here," she says, giving me three extra bandages. "Just in case."

Dad and I thank her as we walk out of the tent and hit the beach, which has now turned sunny and hot.

13

"So how was your little…adventure?" Cerel stands there with a smug look on his face. Must've heard from Armand and Dominic. I knew those guys could never keep a single thing to themselves. I ignore him, sit on one of the beach chairs under the umbrella and pull a turkey sandwich out of the cooler. When I bite into it, it actually tastes good. That's a happy surprise. I haven't had much luck with food this weekend, but this sandwich is quite satisfying. Soft cheese and meat blend with a nice crunchy pickle and fresh tomato. Yummy.

Cerel sits down on the boogie board by the umbrella and watches our moms go into the water.

Just as I finish the last bite of my sandwich, Baby Sara crawls out from under my chair. Startled, I jump and almost step on her. I didn't even know she was there. I plop back down and try to relax. She attempts to climb up onto my lap, so I help her. Well, at least she's not here to bug me or make fun of me, like everyone else.

Ew. Something smells bad. I look at her, and she laughs...and smells.

"Cerel..." I say in horror. "Your little sister just...umm...how do I say this?"

"Pooped her pants," he laughs. "'Glad she didn't try climbing on my lap."

"Well," I say. "Now she is." I put Sara on his lap, and he yelps. I smile. "Your sister, not mine."

"Can you go get my mom?" He holds baby Sara at arm's length away from his body, and his voice sounds shaky and disturbed. Finally, I've got him for once. Oh, what a wonderful feeling.

I shrug with a smile. "You already heard about my foot, so you know I can't go into the water. And she's in too far to hear me yelling from shore."

"Fine…fine." He's clearly frustrated.

"Really wish I could help," I add with the fakest sincerity ever, as I settle back down into my comfy chair.

He runs to the water and flags down his mother. It looks really funny, because he holds Sara out to one side the whole way. Auntie Heather leaves the water to meet him, but she refuses to take Sara even though Cerel keeps trying to shove the cute and smelly little package into her arms.

They return to the umbrella area, and Cerel looks like he's about to puke. "Now let me take care of that," Auntie Heather says and plucks baby Sara from Cerel's still outstretched arms. He collapses onto the sand to my left and stares up at the sky with his dark sunglasses covering his eyes. I just look over at him, say nothing and savor the moment. I don't feel like I need to say anything. Just soak it in, Chloe. Just soak it in.

As if he can sense me looking at him, Cerel turns his head enough to look at me sideways from under his shades. I laugh, and he laughs too.

"I wish had a phone," I say. "I'd make a million dollars with a viral video of you running while holding a pooping baby."

"I'd never show my face again," he says, turning away and looking upward to the sky. "But I had no choice. I can't take that smell."

We just sit there silently. I can see from the side that he has closed his eyes and seems to be listening...just listening to the sounds around us. So, I close my eyes and listen intently.

The waves aren't pounding the shore as hard today. They actually make a smooth and gentle rolling sound when they hit, followed by a slight 'swoosh' when they pull back to the water. After about ten seconds, I start to hear other sounds mixing in with the waves. As the sounds surround me, I get lost in them and begin to nod off to sleep. Just as I'm about to completely doze off, Auntie Heather's voice wakes both me and Cerel, who had apparently also nodded off for a minute.

"Cerel, wake up. Wake up," Auntie Heather says while still holding baby Sara. We both jump a bit, because the horrible smell is still there.

"You haven't changed her yet?" Cerel asks in a disgusted voice.

"I can't find the diapers. Must have left them at home," she replies. "Where's that shovel you and Faegan use when you build sand castles?" Cerel and I look at each other and try not to gasp. It doesn't matter that he's wearing sunglasses, I know exactly what he's thinking and what he's about to say.

"Wait a minute," he says, "You're not planning to use my shovel to bury Sara's poop?"

"Yes," Auntie Heather says with an annoyed tone. "That is what I am saying."

"Can't you just dump her bathing suit into one of the trash bags?"

"No. I need to wash it and put it back on her."

"What?! No way!" Doesn't she have a diaper anywhere? There's gotta be one somewhere in all these bags."

"No. There isn't," she snaps back. "Now just give me the shovel."

Cerel and I stare at her. Then, we look at each other and I give a little 'eek' sound. It's my way of supporting him without going too far. But actually, my reaction bugs Auntie Heather, and she gives me a quick glance, then turns back to Cerel.

"Now," she says to him.

He makes one last attempt to stop the imminent madness. "Mom, we know people around here. We're gonna get a reputation as the trashy family. Can't you just bring her home?"

"Now," She commands through gritted teeth.

He gets up, goes around the back of the beach umbrella and comes out with the shovel. He hands it to Auntie Heather and says, "Don't bother giving it back."

I do nothing but close my eyes.

14

"Oh my God. Oh my God. Oh my God!" Cerel yells. "What is she doing?!" I spit my mouthful of chips into the garbage bag and feel as if I might throw up. Auntie Heather is dumping Sara's poop into the hole that she dug just five feet behind our umbrella and is now using the same shovel to close the hole! And now she's putting the same pants back on Sara, who, by the way, has no underwear OR diaper on!

Is this really happening?! Cerel and I watch everyone come out of the water, look at Auntie Heather and what she's done, then approach us with green faces. "Oh gross," I say to him. "Oh, that is so gross." I can keep saying gross, but that still wouldn't explain how gross this is.

Auntie Heather comes back to us with the poop shovel and holds it out to Cerel, who takes a step back and looks at the thing like it's some alien being. "Can you clean this shovel by dipping it in the water for a few minutes?" Auntie Heather asks him with Sara bouncing around again like nothing happened. Easy for her. She didn't have to see everything. I mean, everything.

"Wait... what?" Cerel asks. I would normally laugh at him right now, but I'm so disgusted by what I just saw that I actually feel bad for him. This whole thing is a first. I don't even want to win against him right now. I just want his disgusting nightmare to end. "I'M NOT TOUCHING THAT!" he yells and points to the shovel as if it were the poop itself.

"Cerel," Auntie Heather says. "Please do it, I have to give everybody their lunch now."

"Hold it." His tone of voice is now defiant. "You're going to feed everybody lunch after you just touched the stuff that came out of Sara's butt?" Good point. I have to say, my thoughts exactly.

"Cerel!" Auntie Heather sternly points to the water. He snatches the shovel from his mother's hand and heads that way. I can hear him muttering something that sounds like "Sh-Firg-bast-ick-hole" as he gets further away from us. Everyone else overheard the conversation and suddenly becomes "un-hungry." Then, they all sort of disappear back into the water. Auntie Heather looks puzzled for a moment but then follows them.

So I sit here alone with no book, no friends, no family members...nothing. For a couple of minutes, I keep glancing behind the umbrella at the little area where Auntie Heather buried the 'stuff'. I don't really expect to see anything. But still, isn't beach sand not really solid? What will happen when the tide comes up? Sooo, how about unicorns and other sweet thoughts. I move my chair a few more feet away from the area and decide I'll be nowhere near here during this afternoon's high tide.

I wish I had brought my sunglasses. I'm squinting so much right now that I just close my eyes briefly to avoid the glare. I open them in time to notice a fin sticking out of the water. That's weird. I wonder-…suddenly, people close to the water start screaming "Shark! Shark!" A father runs in, plucks out his two little girls and carries them like luggage under his arms all the way to the boardwalk.

The lifeguards clear the water fast. Two of them drive up and down the beach on a little RV and wave swimmers out of the water. Three more lifeguards swim out to the few people who are too far away to notice the commotion. Wow, you have to be pretty brave to be a lifeguard at a sharky beach. Two of them are girls. They look really cool swimming super-fast and wearing matching outfits. I feel like I'm watching that old TV show about lifeguards (can't remember what it's called, but Dad says it was great). I can't believe how fast the lifeguards cut across the waves to the swimmers and get back to shore.

Mom was right…I should keep taking more swim classes at the "Y". It could definitely help save a life someday. It's just that I was the only girl in my last 'Dolphins 2' class and was always standing in line behind taller boys with barely any clothes on. My face was literally inches from their bare skin. When you're that close, you see all these little moles and things that just gross you out. Eck.

Now what? Behind me, there's a bunch of teenage girly screams. I can tell when they're from teen girls, because they're so much louder and higher pitched than normal ones. And they're meant for attention. What do you know? It's the group of half-naked girls from yesterday. They run around in circles, yelling Oh My God and Shark! Shark!

What? They're on the beach, like a hundred feet away from any water. Could you be any more over-dramatic? I am not looking forward to two more years of this in middle school. Finally, just when things seem calm, we hear the sirens from an ambulance. It pulls into the distant parking lot. I didn't notice before, but lifeguards are pulling an elderly man on a stretcher right past us and up the boardwalk.

One of the half-naked girls exclaims, "Oh my God...the sharks got him! The sharks!"

Seriously? He was sitting down on his towel the whole time. I saw him reading a book just a minute before this whole mess started. He looks about 90 years old, so it could be anything. But I bet she's going to tell all her friends at school how she was in the middle of a shark attack and is lucky to be alive, and how the man next to her got munched and how she was so close that she could hear the teeth sink into his leg bone and... blah, blah, blah...drama.

My parents, Auntie Heather, and Uncle Brygus pack up everything before this place gets even crazier. Baby Sara cries while being carried by Hunter, because she doesn't understand why we all have to leave the water. She struggles to get down. "I watt. I watt!" she yells. She wants to say walk but she still can't pronounce the letter 'k'. "I watt! I watt!" Hunter gives up and lets her 'watt'.

Cerel just struts away like he's the new model for Abercrombie and Fitch. I'm very cheerful since we get to leave, and Armand and Dominic run around as if nothing happened and keep playing on the beach. As we leave, a final thought pops into my head. I hope I'm not blamed for all this. It can't really be me that attracted the shark.

"It's not my fault!" I snap at Cerel. He just gives me a doubting look with his eyebrows raised. Gosh, I really want to smack him.

"But, Chloe," he says, still holding that seriously annoying smile on his face. "Sharks are attracted to blood. And you were dripping tons of it outta your foot."

"Shut Up," I say behind my gritted teeth.

Hunter looks at me from across the picnic table. "Did you cut yourself that badly?"

"Yeah she did," Cerel says. "I saw her. She was at the first aid with her dad, and the nurse was soaking up tons of blood from her foot. Didn't you see her?"

"So? That doesn't mean I attracted the shark. There are lots of people and other fish in that water!" I yell at him, but quickly quiet down when Sara comes to sit on my lap.

"Whatever," Hunter adds as he gets up. "I'm hungry. We never got to eat lunch, and I'm starved. I'm going in for one of those sandwiches."

"Well, bye then," I say back. I turn around and look at Cerel, who looks at me, then his sister, and then back to me. With an eyebrow raised, he just keeps repeating the same pattern.

"What's wrong with you?" I ask.

He keeps studying the two of us. "Since when does she like you so much?"

I flip my bangs out of my right eye. "I'm a very likeable person," I say confidently. "Unlike some people," I add, looking him straight in the eye. Sara jumps up and down on my lap and laughs.

Auntie Heather comes out of the house. "Let's take a walk," she says to us. "Just us three, and let's bring Sara."

"Sara watt!"

I bend over and tie my sneakers.

"Again?" Cerel asks with his eyes fixed on my feet. "Why don't you just go barefoot like normal people?"

"Because. I'm unique. Now get over it."

"I'll say."

15

This has been a really calming walk. It's only disturbed slightly every once in a while when Sara tries to say something. I never realized how many words have a 'K' in them until she tries saying kite and pickle, but they come out "Tite" and "Pittle". Oh well, she's unique, too.

I walk next to Auntie Heather and hold baby Sara's hand. We talk about school and what I've been doing this summer. What have you been doing this summer? For some reason, to me, that is the most common and annoying question in the history of questions. It bugs me so much, and I don't know why. Maybe because it adds all this pressure to my day. If I say "not much," does that mean I'm a lazy kid? If I say I'm doing all kinds of things, will she say I should relax and enjoy summer?

I know how to answer when my Mom's friends ask, because they're 'Asian Tiger Moms' – the kind who sign up their kids for extra math classes after school, make them play piano four hours a day and think the Russian School of Math is a fun summer camp. But Auntie Heather could be either relaxed or tiger mom-ish. I can't tell. So, I say a little bit of both. I tell her about my film-making class, except I talk about how we used computers for it, and I don't tell her about my acting class at all. She seems satisfied with my answer.

We walk past a yellow house, and a big fluffy cat steps out slyly. But it quickly changes its attitude and becomes all friendly. It purrs and brushes its furry body against my leg, shamelessly begging me to scratch behind its ears. I crouch down.

"Does it have a collar?" Auntie Heather asks me. I look at the cat's neck and find a black collar with the name Snowball written on it.

"Yes," I say.

Who would name their cat Snowball while living in Nantucket? I find that seriously disturbing and depressing. Why bring up cold, dark winter thoughts in the middle of the fun, warm summer? I rub the cat's ears, and it sits on the ground as if I were going to stay here all day with it.

Baby Sara looks at the cat and then back to me. She laughs. "Mama," Sara says to her mom. Then she points to the cat. Actually, it looks like she's pointing at me when she blurts out, "Big titty!"

I stop petting the cat, and Auntie Heather just stands still. Cerel bursts out laughing. Auntie Heather lets out a little giggle, but then Cerel starts clapping. "Say that again, Sara! Big what?!" I hate that guy.

Sara starts clapping, too, and points back at the cat. But once again, it looks like she's pointing at me. "Sara lite titteeee!" she bursts out. Cerel laughs harder. Of course, Sara's happy she has an audience, so she keeps yelling it and pointing toward the cat and me.

"Alright," Auntie Heather says to us. "We should get back now so we can shower. I'm sure the others are done by now."

Thank God she broke that up.

Yay! I didn't forget my towel. I didn't forget anything this time. At least, I don't think I did. I look around the shower before turning on the water. I have my towel, clothes and soaps. Good, now I can start.

No, I can't. I want to make the unlockable door lock somehow. I take one of my elastic bands off my right arm and create a large knot that I stretch from the door's hinge to the sliding thingy. There. Now I can actually shower without worrying.

I turn on the water and throw my dirty clothes onto the clothing pile that has stacked up from everyone else who showered before me. Aw, c'mon. I hate seeing people's dirty underwear and all that. It really is disturbing. I've never been the camping or outdoorsy type. In fact, I played sick when we had our sixth grade camping weekend so that I could just avoid all this icky bug-mosquito-dirty-underwear-outdoor shower stuff. But still, my shower goes well…flawless. Ahhh, refreshed, clean and comfy in my new clothes.

I open the door. At least, I try to. I grab the elastic band and attempt to remove it from the door's hinge, but it won't come off. It's too tight. Hmmm. I try to break the elastic, but it's too thick. I also can't untie it, because it's stuck together from the moisture of the shower. So, I put one foot on the wall and pull the door towards me. I can feel the walls shake. Oh, I should probably stop…wouldn't want to tear down the shower walls.

I don't hear anyone outside. I'm definitely alone. I wish Mom or Dad were here. But they're not. Now what? That's a stupid question, because there's really only one way out of here if I want to avoid complete embarrassment. With no walls at the bottom of the shower, I guess I just have to slide under and out. Simple enough. That sounds like a fantastic plan.

I slip my shampoo and soaps under the wall. And now it's my turn. I crouch down and see that the opening at the bottom is a little bit smaller than I had thought. I stand up, relax my shoulders and start wiggling my arms and legs the way professional swimmers do before a race. I even swivel my head around and loosen up my neck. There. I should be flexible and relaxed enough to fit through without a problem.

I lay my towel on the floor so I don't have to rub against the cold, wet ground. Next, I lie on my stomach and slide my right arm through the opening, and then squeeze my right leg through. Now the right side of my body is outside the shower wall while my left side is still inside it. If anyone came across the shower right now, they'd see me looking like a turkey sandwich with half the meet hanging out one side. I slide to the right a little more, easing my way out slowly. Almost there. Almost there…OUCH!

My stomach is stuck between the floor boards and the wall of the shower. It really hurts. I'm probably going to have a large red mark on my midsection when I get out. Suddenly, I hear someone coming near.

"Yeah, that's what she said. Funny, right?" It's Cerel. And who the heck is he talking about? It better not be me. Oh, but if he sees me like this, then he'll really talk it up. I quickly start moving to the right, but my stomach scrapes the wood, and it burns badly.

"That's hilarious," Hunter says. Ugh, he's here, too. Oh great. I try to pull back inside the shower, but I'm too far through now, so I squirm to get out as fast as I can. They're getting closer. I need to keep moving. I just…can't. And here they are. Oh joy.

They have Sara with them. As soon as she sees me - or half of me - sticking out the bottom of the shower, she runs over and squats down giggling. She thinks I'm playing with her, so she swipes her hand at my face. Ow! Right in the eye. I bite my lip to stop myself from screaming at her.

"What the heck?" Cerel asks as he looks at me strangely.

"Are you two just gonna stand there?" I ask. "Ow. Stop!" I yell as Sara twists my nose. Then she jumps up and runs in circles laughing. She's so excited that she spits some drool and spins, then falls on her butt and slaps at the ground in joy. Cerel looks at me and crosses his arms.

Hunter walks forward to help, and baby Sara just points at me. "Titty," she says laughing. Everyone freezes.

"See?! What did I just tell you?!" laughs Cerel and he looks at Hunter.

Then, Cerel really hams it up. He starts rolling on the ground once again and laughs like a lunatic. "I love my sister!"

He rolls over to Sara and kisses her on the head. She throws her little two-year-old hands at him and points her chubby thumb at me. "Toey," she says smiling.

"So…so," Cerel says struggling for air. "She was pointing at you the whole time!"

I stop trying to free myself from the shower and give him a grim look. "She wasn't pointing at me, because she calls me Toey! And she's not meaning it that way! She means that I was holding the ti-!"

Hunter looks at me like I'm crazy. "You were holding the what?"

Cerel starts cackling like a moron. I didn't mean it that way! But here I am, again, with these two and basically talking to myself.

"Are you going to help me out of here or what?"

Hunter walks forward and grabs my feet and pulls.

"Hey!" I yell. "That really hurts! What on earth are you thinking?!"

"Sorry," he says. "But it's not like I've ever done this before."

I roll my eyes and look at Cerel, who sits on the ground laughing to himself. I grab a pebble with my free arm and try to throw it at him. But since my body's stuck, it's a lame throw that only goes, like, six inches. He laughs some more.

"Can you just help me?" I beg.

He shrugs. "Yeah, sure. Why not?"

"Good. Now get over here before Hunter disconnects my leg from the rest of me!"

Boys are so stupid. Not all, but Cerel isn't just stupid, he's so...so, how do I put it? He's so...ugh.

"Alright," Cerel says, taking hold of my right arm while Hunter has my feet. "On three. Three...Two..."

"Stop!" yells Hunter.

"What? Why?" asks Cerel.

"You said 'on three', but then you started with three," answers Hunter.

"So?"

"So, if it's on three, you're supposed to start at one, not three."

"No, you start at three and-"

"Hey!" I yell. "Who cares? This hurts!"

"Oh. Sorry," says Hunter. Then, he looks at Cerel. "Ready?"

"Ready. One..."

Don't you dare mess this up.

"Two…"

My life is flashing before my eyes.

"THREE!"

16

"If it wasn't for me, you would've been stuck there all day," Cerel says smirking.

"Yeah well, when you pulled me out from under the shower, you gave me a large bruise right splat in the center of my stomach." I'm just not in the mood right now.

He rolls his eyes. "You should thank me. And hey, by the way, you never said why you were slithering out the bottom of the shower in the first place. What was that about?"

"I don't wanna talk about it."

"Hmm, suspicious," he whispers, but lets it go.

Hunter steps outside carrying Sara, who giggles and kicks her legs trying to break free. She squirms down his body, then runs over to sit on my lap. "You know how weird you looked?" Hunter asks me.

Sara giggles even though she has absolutely no idea what she's giggling about. She climbs from my knee onto the picnic table and looks down on us. I love how babies can just do whatever they want and not worry at all. She looks around and claps her hands. Then, she just lets herself fall toward me, one hundred percent sure that I'll catch her.

"SHOOT IT!" Dad yells to me. I fall into the ocean without a word. I'm supposed to shoot the large diaper floating above my head, but instead, I get pulled down deep by a great white shark. I have absolutely no idea why, but the gun in my hand turns into the gross poop shovel, so I smack the shark's nose with it. Suddenly, I break free and swim upward.

I see Cerel, Hunter and Faegan about five feet in front of me. I call to them for help. They all turn around and smile. Faegan starts toward me. Too late, the shark bites from below, and blood starts squirting out the bottom of my foot. But I don't feel any pain.

That was a weird dream but it felt so real. It can't be. I touch my foot where the shark bit. It's fine. Yup, definitely a dream. Besides, who shoots a diaper in the middle of the ocean?

My nose is runny again. I know Dad put the tissue box on the floor by the bed, so all I have to do is roll over and…nope. I am NOT rolling over again on this thing. No spills tonight.

17

I wake up Monday morning. Yes! Our last day! But actually, I feel a piece of regret in my mind as I think about it a little more. Maybe it's because I can hear the beautiful sea breeze through my open window or catch the scent of the smooth sand from the nearby beach. Come to think of it, this is a pretty nice place. And, the weekend hasn't been a total disaster like I thought it would be.

I don't hear the usual heavy breathing sounds my parents make when they're sleeping, so I could be alone for once. I lift my head just a bit to see if Armand's in the bed across from me. He's not. Yay! I can rest here for as long as I want. Only one slight problem…my hunger interrupts this peace. Do I go upstairs and eat or lie here a while longer listening to the breeze? My stomach gurgles. Breakfast it is. Clearly, I'm not going to be one of those girls who starves herself. I like eating too much. So I get up.

In the bathroom, I'm struggling to run a brush through my tangled hair. It hurts in some spots, because the knots are really big. When I'm done, I look in the mirror and admire my work. It's not a piece of art or anything, but at least my hair looks good for once.

Every person has one of those days when they feel so good. That's how I feel right now. I bound up the stairs, taking them two at a time and burst through the door that leads to the kitchen. Dad and Uncle Brygus jump a bit in surprise. Dad spills some of his coffee onto the floor. "Geez, Chloe. Take it easy," he says.

"Sorry Dad." I jump two-footed over to him and throw my arms around his waist and hug as hard as I can. I squeeze my head against his shoulder and give him a huge, goofy smile. He kisses my forehead. I keep smiling.

"Um…you can let go now," he says. I release him and stand there blinking with a fake pout and my *what's for breakfast* look on my face.

"Morning, Chloe," Uncle Brygus says to me. I smile very gleefully at him, then turn back to Dad with my pouty eyes.

"Pancakes," Dad says. "Chocolate and strawberry."

"Yay!" I clap my hands like I'm a little baby girl and hug him again.

"Well, this is a different Chloe today," uncle Brygus adds.

"Hormones," responds my dad. "You never know what's coming next."

What a day! Beautiful breeze and beach sounds wake me up. My hair looks good. No pimples. And now I get my favorite choco-strawberry pancake breakfast.

"I have to go to the pharmacy. Do you need anything?" Uncle Brygus asks Dad.

"I'm all set, thanks. Chloe, I need you to cut the strawberries for me, please."

Dad goes over to the fridge, takes out the strawberries, and hands them to me. "Remember," he says. "We're feeding like, eleven people. Oh, and by the way, your mom's making fish."

If I had a drink in my mouth, I'd probably spit it out in surprise. "She's what?"

"I know. I know," he says. "Let's make it fun and treat it like a contest. "Mom's team will cook the Indonesian fishy dishes. Our team will whip up lusciously sweet pancakes, and may the best team win!"

"And who is our 'team'?" I ask.

"Well let's see. There's me and you...and...you and me. That's all we need. We'll win."

Just then, Auntie Heather, Mom and the Filipino lady from next door walk into the kitchen through the side door of the house. Oh my God. I didn't notice in the darkness of last night's cookout, but Mom and the Filipino lady look like sisters...long lost twin sisters. Whoa. Are the Philippines and Indonesia connected or something? I mean, my friend Cate's mother is from Thailand, and our moms look nothing like each other. But these two. If they wore the same clothes, I might actually follow the wrong lady home.

I stare at them for a few seconds and look around to see if anyone else has noticed this bizarre twist to the morning. Dad's got his back turned to them and is mixing the pancake batter.

Then I get this really weird thought. What if Dad doesn't see them together and accidentally gives the Filipino lady a good morning kiss before he realizes she's not Mom? How weird would that be? Would Mom flip out? I think I don't want to know, so I tap Dad's shoulder and whisper in his ear, "They look like twins. Behind you."

He slowly turns his head, then stares at them over my shoulder. His face shows no expression. But when he turns back, he whispers to me, "Wow. Freaky…Twilight Zone freaky." Twilight zone? Oh yeah. Right. It's that old TV series where really strange things happen to people.

Mom, Auntie Heather and the Filipino lady are each carrying two bowls covered by tin foil. I can't see what's inside, but something tells me there's a smelly, fishy reason why they're covered. Mom mumbles something to them and turns to Dad and me. "OK!" she announces. "The real breakfast ingredients are here! Who's ready for us to make the fiss?"

"Nobody will want fiss after my pancakes!" Dad declares and holds up his pancake flipper triumphantly. "Seventeen years here and I still can't get her to pronounce the 'sh' at the end of words."

I laugh, because it's true. But then again, whenever he speaks Indonesian, he messes up...like really badly. I once watched him offend an Indonesian government official by accidentally saying that his son was handsome and has "a very round and short coconut head."

Mom and the other ladies plop their bowls onto the corner of the kitchen floor and step outside. They must be going next door to gather more ingredients.

Cerel comes into the kitchen. "What's up?" he says while nodding his head upward.

Dad turns around with the pancake flipper, splashing batter as he talks with his hands. "Oh, hey Cerel," he says. "We need your help. Chloe and I have to prove to the moms that everyone's gonna eat our pancakes instead of their fish breakfast."

"Fish for breakfast? What kind of-" Cerel starts to ask.

"Never mind about that. It's a really foul-smelling thing," Dad says. "Go around and find out what everyone wants on their pancakes, please. We have chocolate chips, strawberries and whipped cream."

"Yeah," Cerel says. "But I was about to-"

"Great," I say to Cerel as I grab a notepad that happens to be on the counter. "You agreed. Now go." I hand him the notepad and a pencil. He looks confused for a second, but shrugs his shoulders and goes outside to get the orders.

I wash the strawberries. When I'm done, I feel something slap my shoulder. I turn around to see a little pancake batter on my shirt and Dad standing there holding the spatula. "Umm, gross. Do you mind?" I ask.

"I need that first order. Go ask Cerel what it is."

"Sure, but can you not do that again? It's unsanitary and makes my clothes dirty."

He just looks at me blankly. I sigh, then leave to find Cerel. I run onto the front porch and grab my sneakers. They're so comfy. When I get to the picnic table, I find Hunter with baby Sara, Armand, Dominic, and Faegan. But no Cerel. "Do you guys know where that other lunatic is?" I ask them.

"No," Hunter says.

"Nope," Faegan replies.

"What's a lunatic?" Armand and Dominic ask in unison.

"Toey," Sara says, pointing at me.

"Chloe. C-low-ee," I correct her.

"Toey!" she shouts and raises her arms over her head in victory.

"Okay. Toey it is." Great. I wonder how long, like how many months or years, that will be her name for me.

"Alright, thanks," I say to them and run around the back of the house to look for Cerel.

I arrive in front of the boys' bedroom door that faces outside the house. I knock gently at first, but when there's still no answer after five knocks, I yell, "Cerel!" Still no answer. He's got to be here. Where else could he be? I knock even harder, then stop. What if he's on the toilet and constipated or something? Who cares? I knock and knock and knock. He finally opens the door.

"What do you want?" he asks tiredly.

"What do you mean what do I want? You're supposed to be taking breakfast orders."

He looks at me and rolls his eyes like he's about to say something sarcastic, so I cut him off. "Oh shut up and just tell me what your brothers want on their pancakes."

He stares at me without saying anything.

"What?!" I ask in frustration.

"You told me to shut up," he says smiling. "So I shut up."

"I didn't mean it literally!"

He yawns and stretches his arms. "Okay," he finally says. "Dominic wants a chocolate chip pancake with whipped cream on top in the shape of a smiley face and strawberries for the eyes."

"Thank you," I say, clearly frustrated. He closes the door on me. "What about everyone else?!" I yell through the door. No reply. "Hey!" Whatever. I can get Dad started with Dominic's order.

So, I walk back to the front of the house and kick off my shoes as I enter, because they just got all dusty when I ran through the backyard soccer field. I slide across the hardwood floor in my socks and go into the kitchen where I find Dad standing by the counter and holding some strawberries on a plate. He's already chopped up half of them. "Dominic wants a chocolate chip pancake," I say as I step around the moms and their fish bowls. Ew. I try to not look backwards, because Mom, Auntie Heather, and Mom's clone are literally cooking on the floor. They have two portable gas stoves, knives, oils…everything.

To avoid getting grossed out at the sight of raw, skinned fish, I focus on my dad who's already flipping the first pancake. I grab a dish, and less than two seconds later, he gives me the pancake. "This is for Hunter. Auntie Heather gave me his order. What next?" he asks, spinning the spatula.

"Dominic wants a chocolate one with a smiling whipped cream mouth and strawberry eyes."

"Geez. Pretty specific. And?"

"That's all Cerel told me so far."

"C'mon, Chloe! Can't you see the Moms are catching up? We can't just do one at a time."

"But Cerel's being a pain."

He looks at me with disgust. "Chloe, forget about Cerel and just take the orders yourself. And do it fast, or we'll be sitting in front of smelly fish for breakfast."

"Hey, we heard that," objects Auntie Heather in a laughing tone.

I head outside again. I have to get the orders from Cerel, because I'll never remember all the details of each person's order. I'm really bad at that kind of memorization. Besides, he has the pen and notepad, too.

18

I don't have time to keep putting on my shoes and taking them off, so I get up the guts to go barefoot except for the little bandage over my crab cut. I take my socks off, tuck them into the pocket of my shorts and speed walk to the boys' bedroom. When I'm only three feet from the door, I find one of baby Sara's squeaky dolls and pick it up, then knock hard on the door. "Helloo!"

The door opens almost immediately and out comes Cerel. "What now?" he asks.

"The rest of the pancake orders, please." I'm clearly making an effort to be polite.

"Okay, so...you want to know peoples' orders?"

"Yes. I would love to know what everyone wants." I remain calm.

"Wow, so polite," he says. Then he shudders. "You see, this is what scares me when girls go through their 'big stage of life' thing. Their moods change every thirty seconds."

"How would you know?" I ask. "You don't even have any sisters old enough."

He just looks at me and lets his shoulders sag.

I can't take it. "And will you stop doing that?!"

"What?" he asks. He stares down at my hand that holds baby Sara's toy. "What's that for?"

"Just...tell me," I reply.

"Faegan wants a plain pancake."

"And…?"

"And what?"

I stomp my foot on the ground and throw the doll at his feet. It gives a little squeak. Very deadly threat, I know. But it works.

"Armand wants a chocolate chip pancake with tons of whipped cream. I'll have strawberry with the works. Oh here." He hands me the notepad. "Just take it."

"Thanks," I say and turn to speed walk back to the front of the house.

"Wait!" he yells at me, and I freeze, then quickly turn around. "So you're finally barefoot," he says, smiling down at my filthy toes.

"It feels gross."

"Then why didn't you just come down the indoor basement steps? It's faster."

Embarrassed that I hadn't thought of that myself, I have no answer. I just go back to speed walking and straight into the house. I don't bother putting on my cool socks again, because that would ruin them, and they're the only ones I have left. Why didn't I think of the basement steps?

Dad is flipping the pancakes and complaining about the centers being gooey. I'm cutting strawberries like a maniac, while the moms are cooking fish on the floor. So, the floor thing. Yeah, pretty weird. But cooking on the floor happens all over Asia. People seem to be able to crouch down for everything there. They crouch down by the side of the road when they wait for buses, crouch down when they are near bonfires, and yes, crouch down near gas stoves when they cook. They seem so much more flexible than me.

"Hand me the strawberries - quick," Dad says. I give him the strawberries and dry the sweat off my palms. I can feel the pressure, because the fishy smell has started to hang over us, which means they've started frying some already. We're behind schedule. I peek behind me and see one of Mom's fish sitting on a plate on the floor. That's really disturbing. It's not like she only took the tail or something. The head is still on it. Everything. The eyes. Those creepy, dark eyes are looking at me. I feel a chill and get goose bumps.

"Dad. That's nasty over there."

He stops cooking for a moment. "Yeah, I know. I told your mom, and she just...well, never mind." He goes back to the pancake pan.

I look back at Mom and her team to see them cutting open one of the fish heads. Why? Why do

I look? Blood squirts and drips onto the plate underneath, and it's ah… just…oh. Mom and Auntie Heather laugh along with Mom's clone. Auntie Heather's finishing a story she's been telling them, "…and Jenna said it was Hunter's teacher who found it." They all laugh. How do they chat and laugh while they're cutting open a bloody fish head?! Literally, the blood is like some big pool, and the smell of the fish's odor has to bug them, too, doesn't it?

As if reading my mind, Dad says to me, "People love that food, Chloe. I can't take it, but lots of people would take that fish seven days a week over pancakes." Then he scrunches up his face and quickly turns back to his work. I nod and go back to cutting the strawberries. To deal with the thicker air and fish odor, I start taking deep breaths and try to hold them.

Suddenly, I can't do this. I just can't stay in the same room with the saltwater and fish smell. I'll faint if I do. The looks…the smell…the whole deal. This is just too much for me. Call me a city girl, but I have to get outside fast. Dad gives me

Faegan's pancake, and I run out of the house without looking back. I made it! I'm outside. I take deep breaths of the ocean air and feel better almost instantly. "That was so disturbing," I say as I reach the picnic table.

"Huh?" Armand asks.

"Nothing," I say and give Faegan his pancake. I don't want to go back inside, but I have to get everyone to gobble down their pancakes before the fish invasion comes.

I run back into the house. Dad and I are cooking so fast that I can see the beads of sweat on the back of his neck. My feet are getting sticky from all the heat, steam and splatter of various ingredients. It's definitely a good thing that I didn't put my socks back on, or else my little blue sparkles would be covered with sweat and nastiness. I hear someone enter the house through the kitchen door and turn to see Cerel.

"Sup?" he asks. He's wearing a pair of sunglasses with orange shades. He flips his short hair, obviously wishing that it were longer and then tries to be cool as he checks out what the moms are doing. But his cool attitude changes fast when he sees them holding drippy fish guts.

He looks like he's just seen a ghost and runs out of the house, dropping his sunglasses onto the floor. He wanted out of here so fast that he didn't even care about his sunglasses. I know someone's going to step on those, so I may as well save them before we have to hear the whining. I scoop the glasses off the ground, place them on the TV table and rush back to my dad, who has a pancake sitting on the counter next to him. "Quick!" he says. "Give that to Armand!" I grab it and run outside.

Without looking, I toss the plate onto the picnic table and run back into the house. We're so far behind that the three ladies are already frying most of the fish. We have to get our sweet, luscious meal served before the fish doom comes. I find another pancake and grab it without Dad saying who it's for. I run back out of the house and plop it in the middle of the picnic table. Someone will want it.

"Thank-" I hear one of the boys say behind me as I rush back into the house, but I can't hear the rest of his sentence because I'm running like a cheetah.

"I need more strawberries!" Dad shouts as I enter the kitchen. At the fridge, I grab the berries and quickly wash them. I keep on cutting and cutting. I dump the strawberries onto the already cooking pancake in the pan, ignoring my father's hand, which was a signal that he wanted to put them in himself. Next to us, Mom and her group are working feverishly. They still keep most of the heads on even when they're cooking! Gross. Okay, I need to stay focused.

I brush my hair back with my fingers. In front of me, I see a tiny pancake on a tiny plate. It's really, really small. "Give that to baby Sara," Dad says to me. I grab the plate and run out of the house, finding baby Sara sitting on Hunter's lap. I scramble over to them and hand the plate to baby Sara. "Toey!" she says clapping her hands and staring at the little chocolaty delight.

Dominic yells that he wants another with just strawberries. I run inside, and now the kitchen is filling with smoke…a lot of smoke. "One more with strawberries," I tell Dad. The Moms already have a few dishes prepared, and they're spooning soup into bowls to go with the fish! I've got to step it up. I rush over to the counter, making sure to jump over the remaining bowl of raw fish. Nasty! I've seen that thing, like, five times by now and I'm still not used to it.

"More strawberries!" Dad says urgently. I run to the fridge, wash the berries, and start cutting. I cut them so quickly that I leave too much of the nice berry part near the leaves. But oh well, no time. I give Dad the strawberries and find another plain pancake sitting on the counter. I think we should be almost done by now. Wait! No, we need our pancakes! The Moms bring some dishes and rice outside. Oh no! I cut more strawberries at lightning speed. I'm working it so hard that I have to step back away from the counter to wipe the sweat from my face. But as I do…I feel a sudden cold, slimy thing grab my foot hard. I look down.

19

Gross.

Oh my. So gross. EW! Oh my God. I'm gonna throw up. I might faint. Seriously. I'm going to die.

My left pinkie toe is stuck inside a fish's eye! I'm gonna faint. I'm gonna puke. But I don't faint or puke. I whisper a yell instead. "Daaaad. Please help!"

It's so gross. Gross, gross, gross. It's so gross. Dad doesn't turn around. What do I do? What do I do? Eeek! It's so gross. I can feel the squishy-ness of it and how deep my foot has sunk into its face. My toe has actually penetrated deep into the eye. WHAT IF MY FOOT GOES SO DEEP THAT I CAN FEEL ITS BRAIN?

"Dad!" I whisper yell again, not wanting Mom to hear. But he's cooking like crazy. "Dad!"

Finally, he turns around. "What, Chloe?!" Can't you tell that I'm trying to-…oh no!" He sort of gags as he looks at my fish-covered foot. "How did you do that?!"

"I didn't. Mom left it on the floor!" I yell in a whisper again. "Please help me. I don't think I can take this. I'm gonna pass out."

He tosses his pancake flipper onto the counter, then bends over to grab the fish. "You're gonna pull your foot away when I say so. Ready?" he asks.

"Wait. What about my foot? What if the eye hole cuts me?! It feels boney."

"It's not gonna cut you. It's smooth. Now ready?"

"Are you sure it's smooth? You said there were no sharks at the beach, but there were."

He has this really bad habit of always trying to make things seem like they're not a big deal until after they finish happening. Then, he later admits we were in real danger. A raccoon was going nutty in our backyard when I was little, chasing around Armand and me. Dad jumped out of the tool shed with a net and a chainsaw, claiming he was "just gonna fool around with it." He said raccoons loved this kind of game. Three years later, I learned what a rabid animal is and how that raccoon could have really hurt us.

"Are you sure?" I ask.

"Piece of cake," he replies. "Ready?"

What choice do I have? I nod my head.

"Okay," he says, "One…two…three!"

I pull. My foot comes out, as if the fish were eating it. Pieces of fish guts splatter all over the floor and an eyeball lands by my feet.

"AH!" I scream. There's blood all over my foot. "You said it wouldn't hurt! You said! My foot's bleeding!"

"It's not your blood. It's the fish's," he calmly replies. "Now stop screaming. Your Mom will flip if she sees this."

Too late. I just blew my cover by panicking and yelling. People rush into the house. Great. In come Mom, Auntie Heather, Hunter, Armand,

Dominic, Cerel, Faegan, baby Sara, and the clone of Mom.

"MY FISS!" Mom yells as she looks at the guts on the floor.

Of course she cares about the fish. Because it makes a lot more sense to feel bad for the already dead fish instead of comforting your daughter who is now scarred for life.

"It was on the floor!" I reply. "Who leaves a dead fish on the floor?!"

Dad nods. "She has a point, Ria," he says while looking at Mom.

Mom looks furious. I don't know why she is. I should be the one who's furious. And look at that horrifying eyeball stuff sitting right next to my left big toe.

"I needed that to cook," she says angrily.

The boys have been cracking up laughing in the background since they came in and saw the fish pieces all over the place. Baby Sara tries to walk over to me. Dominic, Armand and Cerel start pointing and laughing. Then they all start egging on Sara to grab the eyeball by my foot. "Pick up the eyeball, Sara! Sara, can we have that?! Get it, girl!"

"Cerel!" Auntie Heather yells. "Be quiet!"

"Sara!" Hunter gasps. Too late, Sara clutches the eyeball. "That isn't a toy!" He shakes her hand, and the eyeball flies out, then splats and sticks to the wall. Well that just sends the four others into a hysterical fit of laughter. Armand, Dominic, Faegan and Cerel are whooping it up like a bunch of hyenas.

"Me watt!" Sara screams. But Hunter takes her outside as she kicks wildly at him. He gives one quick glance back at the eyeball with a puzzled look on his face. "I'll wash her outside, Mom!" he yells as they go out the front door.

I look back at my mom. She's really, really mad. I've never seen her this way. It's lucky we're guests in someone else's house, because she can't lose her mind and flip out completely. She wouldn't want to embarrass the family.

"Clean dis up now," she says super angrily. "Thanks to you, dere's fiss all over Auntie Heather and Uncle Brygus's house." When she gets ripping mad, her English pronunciation becomes really bad. I think about correcting her out of spite but decide that will make things much worse.

Still, I have to defend myself. "Okay, first of all, if you never set the stuff up on the floor…"

"Don't talk back to me! The only reason why I set up on the floor was because you and your dad took up all the space on the counter. It's just pancakes. They are so easy. Not like fiss tradition. Now you clean this mess."

I knew it. See? It's a tradition. What makes that more important? Why can't chocolate pancakes be a tradition? Aren't fish only a tradition for breakfast, because there were no pancakes around a thousand years ago?

"Fine," I say. "I'll clean it up, but I have to clean my feet first. They're contaminated."

"Good," she snaps. "I'm so sorry, Heather. Chloe can be so bad." Then, looking at me, she adds, "So bad."

Auntie Heather walks out with Mom, patting her on the back as she does. The Filipino clone lady stands and stares awkwardly for a moment, then follows them. It's like I'm some kind of evil beast who jumped into the room and started squishing fish and children or something. I'm the victim! I head outdoors to wash my foot in the shower, and as I walk, my left foot still feels like it's stuck in the fish's head.

20

The feeling won't go away. As soon as I get outside, I find all five boys sitting at the table. "How's your foot?" Faegan asks mockingly.

"Stop talking," I reply.

"FISH FEET! FISH FEET!" Armand and Dominic yell while pointing at my foot. "It probably smells a lot!" Armand says excitedly and points at me.

"Did you just call me an *it*?"

"Yeah," Armand and Dominic say in unison.

"Whatever," I mutter. Identical morons.

Cerel sits up. "So first you fall off the mattress and get your head stuck in a fan, then you wake up everyone in the middle of the night, you get stuck in a shower, and now you try turning into a fish. This is gonna be awesome when I tell everyone back home."

"You're a jerk," is my only comeback.

Pretty soon, all the boys are laughing, and baby Sara is clapping her hands together. Great. So glad I can keep the whole gang amused. I walk away, needing to go clean my 'fish feet'.

At the back of the house, I approach the outdoor shower. I step in and turn on the water, put in my left foot, then my right. The water is really cold, but it feels good. I'm surprised that the soap washes the smell off so fast. That's a relief. Clean again, I skip back toward the picnic table, trying to appear like I'm unbothered by everything that just happened. Dad's sitting there now with Uncle Brygus, Cerel and Hunter.

"Hey fish feet," Cerel says to me as I sit down on the bench next to him. I don't want to sit in this spot. But, being beside Cerel means I won't have to look him in the eye every time he makes a childish joke about the fish or yesterday's shark disaster.

"Did everyone eat except me?" I ask Dad.

"I didn't," Uncle Brygus says. "I've been craving your mom's Indonesian food." Cerel and Hunter discover a white hair on Cerel's head and start freaking out about it.

"The only people that ate were Faegan, Dominic, and Armand," Dad replies. "You missed Sara's little pancake flinging episode. We lost some over the wall." He gestures toward the fence that separates the picnic table area and the hedge that backs up to the street. "Your mom and Auntie Heather are making the soup. Which reminds me, I should get our few remaining pancakes before they become 'Sara Frisbees'."

He goes with Uncle Brygus while I'm left with Hunter and Cerel once again. Since the Dads are gone, I take their spots across from the two brothers.

"You let her throw our pancakes onto the street?" I ask accusingly.

"Not me," Cerel says defensively. "He's in charge of Sara."

"Not all the time," argues Hunter. Then he points to my face. "How'd you get that red mark on your cheek?"

"There's also one on your collar bone," Cerel says.

"I fell in the shower yesterday, remember? You only helped me out."

"How do you fall in the-?" Hunter starts to ask before Mom bursts out of the house.

"FISS IS HERE!" The three of us look up and find our moms and the clone standing at the front door with a bunch of plates. They come to the table and put them right in front of us.

"AH!" Cerel panics and pushes back from a plate to his left that has a fish head on it. "Do you just eat it like that?!" he asks.

"Not me," I say.

Cerel and Hunter use their shirts to cover their noses from the smell. But even doing that, the odor goes through the fabric. I'm telling you, it's an odor so strong that it once traveled all the way upstairs, into my room and woke me from a deep sleep. That was after I had closed my door the night before and sealed the opening at the bottom with a towel. Keep in mind, our kitchen is pretty far away from the stairs. But still. It's like some evil fog from a horror movie. You can hide, barricade your doors or try whatever you want. It's going to get you.

"Are you ready to try the fish?" Aunt Heather asks.

"No, thank you," Cerel says without thinking twice.

"Oh please," Auntie Heather says to him. "You guys are such spoiled kids who don't try anything new. At least try this. You'll be surprised."

"But it's a head!" he demands. I've got to agree with him. It is a head. And really, isn't that saying enough?

Dad comes out, holding his breath and carrying a few plates of pancakes. He always tries to put on a good show, but I know he can't stand the fish smell either. I mean, he eats fish, but not fishy smelling fish. He's more of a haddock and crab cake kind of eater. But Uncle Brygus seems to be the total opposite. He's smiling and taking deep sniffs of the fishy-fish. Then he licks his lips as he eyes the rest of the food on the table.

"Here you go," Dad says, handing me my pancake and a fork. Then he does the same for Hunter and Cerel. The four of us sit at one end of the picnic table while the three moms and Uncle Brygus sit at the other end. We're squished together so tightly on our end that Cerel's left arm is literally in my rib cage. We're trying to huddle over our dishes of pancakes to keep the fish odor off them.

"Oh come on, guys," Uncle Brygus says laughing as he bites into a piece of his fish head. "This is a unique feast."

Hunter shivers and a piece of his pancake falls out of his mouth. "I just don't like fish," he says after taking a bite of his beautiful chocolate pancake with strawberry pieces dripping out the sides. "This is more…me," he adds and points his fork at his pancake.

"Yeah Dad," Cerel says as he moves his arm, causing it to go even deeper into my ribcage. "That stuff is so…"

"Just stop," Auntie Heather says to him. "You both need to become more open to different things."

"Chloe, too," adds Mom.

I grunt, because (a) I think I'm open to too many things, and (b) my right side hurts, and I think it's bruised.

Suddenly, Dominic and Armand come running to the table with water guns and start squirting Hunter, Cerel, my dad and me.

"Dominic!" Uncle Brygus hollers.

Dad follows with, "Armand!"

"Armand," Mom says, "come try the fiss."

Armand shrieks as she puts a piece of fish on her fork and goes towards his face. He and Dominic run to the backyard, and she gives up. Now, if I had done that, I'd be in trouble for being a rude guest. But not our wittle baby Armand.

21

"So," Uncle Brygus says. "While I was out, I stopped at the harbor and arranged for us to do some sailing today. And I already paid, so that's that."

"Wait," Dad says, "I have to pay, too."

"John, I got it," Uncle Brygus assures Dad.

Dad tries to argue. "No, no, no. we're not going sailing if..."

I stop listening. Mom and Dad are always nice about this stuff. So this goes on for another couple of minutes. No I'll pay, and it's my turn. By the time they finish with their little argument (by the way, Uncle Brygus won) I finish my pancake. That was satisfying...much more satisfying than a fried fish head with the eyeballs falling out.

"So you guys coming?" Uncle Brygus asks everyone.

"No," Auntie Heather says, "I'm pretty beached out."

"Me, too," Mom says. I think Mom really wants to go but is just saying no to stay with Auntie Heather.

"Sure," Dad says.

"I'm in!" Hunter chirps. He seems pretty excited.

"Yeah," Cerel says casually as he sips his iced tea. "Sure, I'll go."

"Umm," I say. "Sure."

It might not be that bad. I mean, I won't really have to do anything. I'll sit on a chair, feel the nice sea breeze and chill with an iced tea or something. Yeah, I like that. And sail boats are pretty big, so I'll have plenty of space to relax. Plus, I've never been.

"I'll go ask the other boys," Uncle Brygus says as he steps back into the house. I hope they say no, because I don't want them following me around the boat and getting in my face the whole time.

"They said no," Uncle Brygus informs us as he comes back to sit down. Yes! A big sailboat with only the older kids and dads. This could be good.

"OH!" Mom says to Uncle Brygus. "I forgot to tell you. Armand's breathing has mostly cleared up, but he still snores once in a while."

Uncle Brygus is a doctor who helped Armand when he had a blocked throat in June. I guess he's an expert about kids' ears, noses and throats. He's always giving speeches in cool places around the world, like Paris and Rome. Dad says it's because big medicine companies want his advice about new ways to cure kids.

"How often does he snore now?" Uncle Brygus asks Mom.

"About one night per week."

"Well, that's a big improvement. It may never stop completely. However, there's a new medicine that-"

Mom's clone cuts him off. "Oh, my boys snore when little. All little Philippines boys snore. All my family. You give him peach bath and ginger tea at night, then no more snore. "

"Umm," Uncle Brygus sounds confused. "It's not really that simple. His case has some-"

"And no cheese for him," the clone continues.

"Yes, true, cheese can cause mucus build up," agrees Uncle Brygus. "But his issue-"

"Wow, really?!" Mom says excitedly to her clone. "I have ginger tea at home."

"Medicine come from Asia plant anyway," says Mom's twin.

"I know!" Mom says all excited. "We get healthy naturally back home, but drug companies come take our plants and herbs, and then make us pay."

Uncle Brygus looks totally confused. He whispers something to himself that I can't hear. What just happened? That lady is not a doctor. I thought Dad said her family manages a restaurant on the island. Uncle Brygus is actually world famous for this stuff.

"Oh yeah…," Mom says as if she's realizing something. I pour myself some iced tea and take a sip of it.

"So, you take my advice?" the clone asks.

"Of course!" Mom says. Then she turns to Dad. "Honey, we should stop at *Bed, Bath & Beyond* tonight and pick up peach bath soap. I like natural Asian herbs instead of medicine."

I almost choke in surprise and accidentally drool a little iced tea onto my lap. Did she really just say that? He's the doctor. You know what, I'm not gonna bother. This isn't my problem. Cerel and Hunter stare at the iced tea drops I just drooled and which are now headed down my leg.

"What?!" I whisper to them.

They keep on staring, and I look at my dad. He looks at Mom and blankly says, "Sure."

I turn back to Uncle Brygus, who takes in a deep breath and closes his eyes. Then I turn to look at Mom's clone. She's picking at a fish bone, unaware of what's going on, while Cerel and Hunter continue to stare at me.

"I'm going to stroll the neighborhood for a bit," Uncle Brygus says to us. "You guys should get ready while I'm gone."

"Sounds good," Dad says and joins Uncle Brygus.

"That was some very satisfying fish," Auntie Heather says, rubbing her stomach.

"Did you like it?" Mom asks.

"Yes, I thought it was delicious."

"Because I liked it!" Mom adds happily.

22

"We're back!" Uncle Brygus announces upon entering the house. I look up from The City of Bones and fix my bathing suit, which is now my spandex pants and YMCA shirt.

"I'm ready," I tell my dad.

"Did you already put on sunblock?" he asks. I nod. "And I think Cerel and Hunter are waiting outside," he continues. So I go outside to join them.

"But it was gross!" Cerel yells at Hunter as I near them.

"Yeah," Hunter replies, "but you shouldn't be so rude about it."

"Gosh Hunter, you're such a nice person," Cerel mutters and folds his arms.

I join them at the table. "When did you get here?" Cerel asks.

I roll my eyes. "Two days ago."

We all sit there for a minute, glancing back and forth and not really having anything to say. Maybe because we've talked about everything we have in common during the last forty-eight hours of our non-stop togetherness. "Where's my dad?" Cerel asks frustrated. Just as I'm about to answer, he runs into the house. And since Hunter and I have nothing to talk about, Hunter seems to panic and leaves to join Cerel after an awkward pause.

So I'm left alone. That's actually a good thing since I want to check on my foot. Does it still have the fish smell? I think it might, even though it didn't right after I washed it. I can still feel the sensation of the eye socket gripping my toe. With no one around, this is a good time to check.

I lift up my foot, bring it to my nose and take a deep sniff. Suddenly, I get the feeling that I'm being watched. I Look up and see the neighbors have magically appeared from around the side of the house. Out of nowhere. NO! Why do they always have to see me when I'm doing something embarrassing?

They all stare at me for a few seconds and then continue on their way into the house without saying a word. I just sit there with my jaw hanging open. I want to say something, anything, to explain why my foot is practically in my nose and why I'm clearly taking deep sniffs of it. But I panic and say nothing. It's ten seconds of pure humiliation. Their silence is worse than if they were making fun of me.

"Don't worry. This will be fun," Uncle Brygus says as he drives us along the shore road. It's just me, my dad, Hunter and Cerel in the car with him. Dad's sitting in the front, Hunter and I in the middle, and Cerel in the back. I haven't listened to a single word anyone has said since the foot-sniffing episode twenty minutes ago. Thank God we're off to our little sailing adventure. The thought that has been rushing through my brain since my latest embarrassment is this: When I smelled my foot, I thought no one was there. And I know there wasn't. So, how did they get there so fast?

"We're here!" Uncle Brygus says excitedly. He must really like sailing. I already know how he loves nature. Actually, he's a total nature freak. Literally, he'll find something as small as an acorn, then go on and on about the way it got there, which plants are its relatives and all this other acorn trivia my science teacher would never know.

There was this one time when they came over to our house, and since we live right next to a state park, Dad said that we should take a walk with their family. But as soon as we stepped foot into the forest, Uncle Brygus found a speck of moss and made some big speech on why it looks light green in some spots, how it absorbs water, and why most animals won't eat it. We couldn't walk ten steps without stopping to get a science lecture. It took four hours to walk two miles.

I get out of the SUV behind Hunter and then stand next to my dad as he puts his shoes into the car. "Why are you taking them off?" I ask. "We're going onto a boat, not a beach."

"Well I…" Dad starts, but gets cut off by Uncle Brygus. "In the event the boat tips over," Uncle Brygus says. "Also, shoes don't help when you're on a boat, and the laces can make you trip, causing you to fall. And that's where invisible currents come in. Now, you're probably thinking that currents have nothing to do with it, especially slow ones, but…"

I stop listening after I hear the word 'but'. I look over at Cerel. He's standing with his arms crossed and his sunglasses back on, yawning widely as his dad continues the lesson. Dad and Hunter are just leaning against the car and nodding in agreement occasionally, just so that Uncle Brygus thinks that they're listening.

"And did you know that if a fish eats something with a disease," Uncle Brygus says, "it'll keep on-"

"Dad," Cerel says calmly at first. But then he gets really annoyed. "DAD!"

Uncle Brygus looks at him. "What?"

"We did come here for a reason, and it wasn't to learn about how jellyfish and palm trees may come from the same part of the world. It was to go sailing."

"Right," Uncle Brygus says, realizing what just happened. Then he looks at me. "You are going to take your shoes off, aren't you?"

"Oh, well…er…you know, I think I'll… umm." I mean to say no, but he keeps looking at me like I'm a little girl who doesn't understand the world of sailing, so I give up. "Yes," I say as I throw my sneakers into the car and close the door.

"I didn't come here with any shoes on," Cerel mockingly says to me.

"Good for you."

"Alright, let's go," Uncle Brygus says cheerfully.

We walk past a few large sail boats. I wonder which one it'll be, because the three that I just saw are really nice. Like, top notch nice. On the side of one of them are inscribed bold silver letters, THE BIRDY. I don't know why it's called that, but it's a beautiful boat. Actually, it's a sailboat, which just makes me even giddier because that might be the one that we're riding today! I can see that the deck is made of this shiny wood that was probably pretty expensive. And what makes me even happier is noticing that on the deck are a bunch of beach umbrellas and chairs. I see a small table with a beach umbrella over it. That is the perfect place for me right now. I could just imagine sitting on one of those chairs and being shaded by a purple beach umbrella as I sip my delicious iced lemonade.

I keep staring at the boat in amazement and don't realize where I'm going, then slam right into Cerel's back. "Sorry," I mutter under my breath. Nearby, Uncle Brygus is talking to some blonde dude in a red bathing suit. I wonder why, whenever I'm at a beach, surfing competition, a ski place, or anything that is like an X-Games sport, the workers are always these laid back, slender guys with blond, curly hair and are like, "Aye, mate." It's starting to freak me out.

"Let's get to our boat!" Uncle Brygus shouts. We all climb into a little dingy with a motor on the back. It's what these blond-haired dude workers use to escort people to their sail boats. Wow, this is the real V.I.P treatment. Our boat must be one of those with the huge sails sitting near the mouth of the channel, far from the beach.

We're only on the dingy for a minute when the engine stops next to another little dingy. "Okay! This is our boat!" I look up to find Uncle Brygus standing in front of a small boat, bathtub actually, that looks just like our dingy but with a small pole sticking up high at the front. No, can't be. This boat is small…like really small. The picnic table might be bigger than this.

"Seriously, Dad?" Cerel asks with his arms crossed sternly.

"What now?" Uncle Brygus asks, clearly annoyed by his son's question.

"What do you mean 'what now'? That thing is so small."

For once, I'm glad Cerel's here. Glad that I'm not the one who says she's horrified by our choice. What's more horrifying is that we were so close to THE BIRDY, that beautiful, clean, brand new dream boat.

"But Dad," Cerel whines, "I thought Mr. Brenton said that we could borrow his boat."

"And which boat is that?" asks Uncle Brygus.

Cerel drops his arms by his sides and rolls his eyes. "Only the most expensive boat on the island!"

"Huh?" Uncle Brygus looks at him blankly.

Cerel yells, smacking his forehead, "THE BIRDY!"

My jaw falls open. We had the chance to ride on the best boat on the island of Nantucket? But instead, we're going sailing on this…this…thing?

"John," Uncle Brygus says to my dad as he nods his head towards the boat. "Help me position it so we can jump in and start sailing."

Dad looks at the boat and hesitates, then he goes to help Uncle Brygus as Cerel, Hunter and I stare at the old tub and shake our heads in disbelief. We wait for a few minutes until our dads are finally done moving the 'boat' and we're ordered to get in. I mean, it was really nice of Uncle Brygus to do this for us. And I don't want to seem spoiled or princessy, but I'm really not sure if we'll actually fit onto the boat. It's that small.

"Hold on. I'll go in first," Uncle Brygus says to us.

"I'll help you get in," Dad says. "It's kind of tall, and I once hurt myself getting in a-"

"Don't worry," Uncle Brygus says proudly, "I'm an expert. I do this all the time. Right guys?"

Cerel and Hunter look up from an argument they're having about who will sit where. "Uh, yeah Dad," Cerel replies, obviously not knowing what his dad was talking about.

Even though the boat is small, I'm glad that we have a guide who actually knows something. No offense to my dad or anything, but there is no way in my life that I would ever have him as my captain on a sail boat. He doesn't even know how to turn a canoe. I was on one with him and some of my friends in the middle of a lake last November. He turned it the wrong way and dumped us all into freezing cold water. Good thing it wasn't summer, because that water has leaches everywhere.

Uncle Brygus puts his right foot over the side of the boat and then starts to bring up his left. But things don't go so well after that. He stands on one of those seat-thingy parts of the boat and attempts to hop on one foot to grab some rope. But when he does, he trips. No, he doesn't trip. He face plants, right splat into the center of the floor. And it's not like his whole body fell flat on it. His right leg is, like, stuck in some net that was under the seat thing.

Dad stares at him for a second in shock, because he hit the floor with a huge thud. "You alright?!" Dad asks.

"Yeah, he's fine," Cerel says casually. I don't know why he's so calm. (A) His own dad just fell face first into a boat and might have broken his nose or something, and (B) that's our guide. The one who's supposed to know what he's doing! I'm not getting on a boat when our guide can't even board the thing without getting hurt.

And it's not like we're sailing in some tiny little bay in New Hampshire. We're going into the open ocean! And I mean the ocean with all of the jellyfish, sharks, huge ships and stuff. The one where if we go too far out and get lost, we might be attacked by a bunch of flesh eating creatures. Not the ocean where you see a bunch of babies floating around on their toys and sucking their thumbs. The dangerous one with huge squid the size of a truck!

"Ow," I hear Uncle Brygus mutter as Dad helps him up.

"Are we still doing this?" I ask nervously.

Hunter looks at me like I'm an idiot. "Of course we're still doing this!"

"Well, I just thought…" but he stops me.

"Who doesn't want to go sailing?!" he adds with a disgusted tone.

"Umm…I guess you could say that I don't really feel comfortable," I try to say.

"It's so fun!" He practically yells.

"Dude, you should just chill," Cerel says to him.

"Did you just call me 'dude'?" Hunter asks, raising an eyebrow.

I ignore their little brotherly argument and go back to my real concern. I'm truly worried that we're about to go into the middle of a huge, endless ocean on something barely bigger than my bed and with no motor.

"Alright guys!" Dad yells to us. "Hop in!"

23

My stomach hurts. I know I'm sea sick, because I would never normally lean my head against a wooden board to comfort myself. Hardly a soft pillow. Dad is sitting next to me and helping Uncle Brygus fix the sail with Hunter. Yeah, fix the sail as we move out to sea. They accidently ripped it, and now there's this giant slice in the center. We contacted the employees down at the beach through the radio, but it turned out they had no more boats or sails to lend us.

"Bend down, fast!" Uncle Brygus yells to me. "Huh?" I start, then quickly realize why he said that. This wooden pole comes flying towards my head, and I bend down just fast enough before it can crush my skull. Geez!

"That was a close one," Dad says laughing and then turns to me. "This is getting fun, isn't it?" he asks as he playfully punches my arm. I groan.

He does know that I'm sea sick. In fact, I already told him three times, but he's acting as if I never said anything.

"You should try steering the boat," Uncle Brygus says to me. Didn't he just face plant into the floor a few minutes ago? How is he so hyper after something like that?

"I don't think she's feeling well," Dad says to him while patting my back like I'm a dog. You think?

Sometimes, just sometimes, I feel like my parents don't listen to me. Like that one time when I told my dad that the bus for school was going to be at our house any minute, and he's was like, "Relax, you need to stop worrying. It was late last time anyway." So how did that go? Well I'll tell you. My brother and I ended up missing it and had to hike to one of the other stops. But no one else was there, and at the time, I had a wedgy. So I hid behind a bush and fixed my pants and told Armand to stand by the road so that the bus driver could see us. He stood out there, and everything was going well until he said that he had to tie his shoe and bent down. And when the bus finally came, it turned out the bus driver couldn't see us, so we had to run around the entire neighborhood, in the middle of the road, until the driver realized that we were supposed to be two of her passengers. My point is that my dad can be terrible at listening, and it really isn't helping today.

"Dad? Can I sit on the-" Cerel asks, but gets cut off by Uncle Brygus who seems to know what Cerel's about to ask.

"Sure," Uncle Brygus says. Cerel gets up and sits on the edge of the boat by my head. Yes, this boat is so small that the back of the boat is literally right next to the front.

"You should really try steering the boat," Hunter says cheerfully to me. I grunt at him. But

Dad takes the opportunity to hand me a piece of rope.

"Yeah, Hunter's right. Here ya go!"

"What is this for?" I ask. But once again, I barely have time to react.

"Quickly!" Uncle Brygus yells to me. I don't know what to do. I'm just holding a rope for some reason. But then I see the large boat coming toward us.

"Pull it!" Dad, Hunter, and Uncle Brygus shout at the same time. So I do what they say and pull the rope. Only, nothing happens.

"You're so weak!" Hunter screams at me. This wasn't even my idea! These guys do know I'm sick.

Out of frustration, I throw the rope at Hunter. I probably shouldn't have done that because the huge boat comes closer to us, and everyone screams. But I don't. I just feel like crap. I don't even have the energy to scream in fear. But I am petrified of that boat hitting ours. It is just about to crush us when the driver sees the situation and turns fast to the left. Oh my God that was close! I breathe deep and hope this trip will end soon.

I go back to leaning my head against the board with my eyes closed. My stomach is killing me, and for some reason, I have some cramps. I think I regret coming today. I could be at home watching TV and sipping some tea. Suddenly, something splashes me. Startled, I look up and see my dad sitting across from me, and like a two-year-old, he just keeps splashing me and smiling. "Will you stop it?" I mutter behind my teeth. I try not to act spoiled and respect my parents, but really?

Cerel sort of lays on the edge of the boat with his sunglasses on and looks completely relaxed. Lucky. I wish I could just chill and not worry about anything, but that won't happen right now, because I just don't trust that we are safe yet.

"Did you guys know that there are jellyfish in these waters?" Uncle Brygus asks my dad and me as if he's thrilled to have monsters surrounding us. I don't respond, but Dad laughs for some reason. I think it's a nervous reaction. He doesn't love the open ocean either. Uncle Brygus takes hold of the rope that I threw at Hunter and starts going on about the ocean and different types of fish. "Now jellyfish are very dangerous. Their stingers can kill you, or at least, cause you tremendous pain. You know, there was this one time when George Washington was asked about crossing the Delaware…"

How the heck did George Washington get into this? I feel another splash of water on me and see Dad and Hunter laughing. Has everyone gone mad?

"Dad!" I whisper yell at him, and he smiles.

"You need to wake up," he says. "You're like a lump on a log." I want to say something, but my stomach does a flip-flop. I really need to get off this thing and stand on shore.

"Dad, I need to throw up," I say quietly.

"Well, don't do it in the boat," Uncle Brygus says to me as he wraps some metal wire around his wrist.

"Dad?" Hunter asks Uncle Brygus. "Can I sit on the bow?"

Uncle Brygus shakes his head. "No, it's too dangerous."

"But Cerel gets to sit on the stern! Why can't I sit on the bow?" His face starts to turn a little red.

Boys are so competitive. And what's a stern, anyway? Oh, never mind. I remember from the canoe. He's just trying to show off his sail boat vocabulary. The stern is the back of the boat, and the bow is the front. Anyone not showing off would have just said the front.

Uncle Brygus throws a rope towards me again. He just won't give up on me.

"Now what do I have to do?" I ask sleepily.

"You're going to pull that when I tell you to," he says as he watches a large boat come our way.

"Wait, like this?" I ask.

"Now!" He yells.

I panic and throw the rope to Cerel, hoping he knows how. Only, he doesn't pull it. He throws it at his dad, who pulls it but accidently pulls too hard, and the rope flies into the water.

"Shoot!" Uncle Brygus yells. "Hunter, grab it!"

From the front of the boat (a.k.a. the bow), Hunter leans over to grab it and...SPLASH! He's gone.

Cerel and I burst out laughing. Hunter's topple over the side is surprising, but Cerel doesn't jump up. In fact, he doesn't move a muscle. Uncle Brygus reacts fast though. "Don't panic! I'll get you!" he yells as he reaches his hand into the water. Cerel and I stretch our heads to see what's going on and watch Uncle Brygus struggle as he tries to lift Hunter back into the boat. But it's just not working.

From my point of view, all I see are three of Hunter's fingers gripping the edge of the boat. Also, Uncle Brygus's upper body is over the side, and he and Hunter keep gasping and struggling. It looks really weird with Uncle Brygus's legs in the boat but his upper body gone. I look beside me, and Cerel is just sitting. He's facing the action, sees the danger, but just finds it amusing.

"Here!" my dad yells to Uncle Brygus, "Lemme help." Dad reaches over the side of the boat next to Hunter's fingers, and I can hear Dad say, "One...two...three!" Suddenly, with a huge jerk, Dad rips Hunter out of the water by the lifejacket. At least, that's what I think he must have done. I can't really see, but this must be how he did it, because Dad falls backward with Hunter flying up out of the water and over Dad's head. But the boat's not wide enough to catch Hunter as he comes down. Instead, as Dad falls back and continues his pulling motion, he actually throws Hunter over the other side of the boat.

The combination of the surprised look on Uncle Brygus's face, Hunter's yelp and my Dad's "holy %#@*!" as Hunter flies into the water again is just too hilarious for words. Cerel and I completely lose it.

For a full minute we are just rolling around laughing, as much as one can roll in such a squished space. Finally, Cerel tries to speak. But it's that kind of speech that you can barely squeeze out when you're laughing so hard you can't breathe.

"It's like...it's like...," Cerel tries to say, but his eyes fill with tears and his breath leaves him..."like we're the only normal ones!" I'm actually convulsing and bent over in tears of stupid joy and start gasping for breath myself. Just then, Uncle Brygus rushes over to help Hunter again but trips over the rope I dropped and falls into the whatcha-call-it-thingy that holds the rope. It's too much for me and Cerel. We lose all control and bang our heads together as we fall back in laughter.

"Sto...sto...stop..." I stammer, but I can't get the words out. Cerel holds his stomach and points at me in silent hysterics. "You...you...look like...BA-HAHAHA!" Tears are pouring down both our cheeks, and I fall against him, because I just can't stand on my own. He wobbles and we collapse onto the deck in unstoppable idiocy and laughter.

We finally get control of ourselves for a second and watch as my dad helps the other two onto their feet. Then we have another laughing fit. We don't even try to get up, because we know we'll fall right back down again. Dad, Uncle Brygus, and Hunter stand over us with angry looks on their faces.

Easily, ten seconds pass before Cerel can control himself enough to say, "What?" But as soon as he does, he and I burst out laughing again. We look like a couple of laughing hyenas surrounded by three angry lions, but it's just too funny to stop. Cerel finally squeezes out words to them through his red face and tears. "You guys…you…looked…like a bunch…of idiots."

Hunter scrunches up his face and gives his brother a dirty look. "It's not funny," he mutters. That's it! Exactly what he shouldn't have said, because it sends Cerel and me into another fit.

I look at Cerel and ask, "Have..? Have you ever…? Crap…!"

He can't believe it. His eyes pop open and he starts hanging off the side of the boat while laughing his butt off and drooling. "Yeah, it was funny!" Cerel says to Hunter, nearly uncontrollably. "You were tryin' to act all swag with your nautical vocabulary, and then, BAM!

You fall right into the water! Twice!" I'm in complete tears at this point.

"Oh, shut up," Hunter says flatly.

Cerel cackles. "Oh! I really touched a nerve. Wait 'til I tell Ryan about this!"

Hunter looks like he wants to punch his brother. "Don't you dare!" he snaps. I'm still choking. But I'm also now holding my stomach, because the laughter has made my cramps worse.

"I'm hungry," Cerel announces to everyone. He and I laugh. Nobody else does.

24

"So, we're gonna meet the others at Lola Burger, right?" Cerel asks his dad and Hunter as we ride in the car.

Nobody answers him.

They're clearly not in the mood to hear anything from him right now.

"What the heck's Lola Burger?" I ask him.

He looks at me in amazement. "You've never heard of Lola Burger? They have the best burgers in the world."

"As good as Fuddruckers?"

"Excuse me?" Cerel asks laughing. "Did you just swear at me?"

"Never mind," I say. My dad and I were always bugged by the name of that restaurant but we like their buffalo burgers. But seriously? Fuddruckers? I agree with Cerel. The name does sound rude.

"Aren't we going to the house and showering first?" Hunter asks. "I have salt all over me."

"No," Uncle Brygus answers. "The ferry departure time is seven, and it's already three-thirty. You can take a quick shower after we eat, while the Taliris get packed."

"I don't need to shower," Cerel announces. "I never fell off the boat."

"I didn't fall off!" Hunter bursts out. "I was reaching for the…the…"

"The what?" Cerel asks sarcastically.

"Just be quiet." Hunter's had enough of Cerel.

Uncle Brygus takes a sharp turn, causing Cerel to fall right out of his seat and slam his face into the car door. "Why aren't you wearing a seat belt?!" Uncle Brygus snaps at him. "Are you crazy?!"

"Well, you never drive like that, and the speed limit here is, like, only ten miles per hour," says Cerel, pushing himself off the car floor. "I thought it was safe. Ya know, like the front of the boat at ten miles per hour." Then he bursts out laughing, and so do I.

I don't know why. It wasn't really that funny a joke. It just hit us the right way. "Will you...stop that?" I ask, still cackling. But he doesn't respond. Instead, he starts snorting in laughter. It's all we needed to set us off again.

It's a nice restaurant. I almost feel embarrassed for wearing my beach clothes to this place. A waitress finds a table for us then lays some menus onto it. "Oh, could you bring five more, please?" Uncle Brygus asks her. "We have more people joining our group soon." She picks up the menus, thinks for a moment, and then leads us outside. I feel better in my clothes when I see a family in bathing suits sitting at the first table on the patio.

This is not like every other restaurant that has regular chairs at the tables. We sit at a large, rectangular table that's surrounded by two couches and a bunch of oversized chairs with large backs and cushiony pillows. My dad, Uncle Brygus and the two boys all sit on one couch while I sit by myself on the other. I was going to take one of the oversized chairs but thought I might sink in too deep. How can I eat like that?

I can see almost everything and everyone in the restaurant from where I am. Cerel turns to his dad. "When's everyone else coming? I'm hungry."

As soon as he says it, we can hear the sound of loud people coming into the room. Armand and Dominic barge in while making weird fart noises with their mouths. Auntie Heather carries a crying baby Sara and gives the waitress an awkward smile as she walks past her. I'm sure the waitress is thrilled to serve our table. Meanwhile, Mom doesn't see the threshold between the main restaurant and the patio, so she stumbles over it and saves herself from falling by grabbing a man's shoulder.

I try to act like I don't know these guys, and when I look up across the table, I can see that Cerel has the exact same expression on his face. Auntie Heather sits next to him and puts baby Sara on his lap without asking his permission. He starts to protest, but his mom just looks at him with a don't complain look on her face.

I bend over and grab a menu from the table and read through the short list. What?! Why would somebody pay eighteen dollars for a cheeseburger? And the rest of the menu? Let's just say I'm not overwhelmed by my choices:

Cheeseburger- $18.00

Avocado hamburger- $22.00

Veggie burger- $16.00

Who pays twenty-two bucks for an avocado burger?! And if that's just like a cheeseburger, but with avocado, then they're charging four dollars for avocado topping. Ouch. And the other side of the menu is even more expensive. I quit reading it and decide to just get a cheese burger, because there is no way on earth that I'll ever eat a veggie burger again. I did it once at school, because that's all they had, and I ended up throwing up in the nurse's office for an hour.

Mom sits next to me and wraps her arm around my shoulders. I try to wriggle free but can't. Across from us, Auntie Heather hugs Cerel hard and then looks at my mom.

"They're growing up so quickly," Auntie Heather says as she sighs and practically strangles him with a tight neck hug.

"I know," Mom replies and pouts. I struggle for breath and finally break free. She gives a little "humph" and reaches for a menu while Armand and Dominic play a round of thumb wrestling. Each time one of them wins, that one gets to bite the other…so barbaric.

The waitress comes to our table a few minutes later and gives Armand and Dominic a strange look, then turns back to us 'normal' people. And when I say normal people, I mean Cerel and me. Because, let's face it, we're the only ones not tripping off boats, strangling their kids or biting one another. We're just normal.

"Do you guys already know what you want?" the waitress asks us. Actually, she looks straight at me and not at anyone else.

"Umm," I say, "I'll have a cheeseburger and…"

Mom cuts me off. "I'll share with her," she says, looking at me.

The waitress raises an eyebrow. "Are you sure? They're not very big burgers. They're more like gourmet burgers."

"Oh, don't worry! She's just a little girl," Mom says. "Plus, we have to keep her healthy…not too much red meat, you know."

"Mom," I mutter. Across the table, I can see Cerel laughing at me.

"You know what?" Mom asks the waitress. "It's our vacation. She'll have a full burger."

The waitress takes in a deep breath. "So you do want her to have a cheeseburger?"

"Yes," Mom replies.

"All to herself?"

"Yes."

"Got it," the waitress says as she jots down something into her notepad. "And what would you like to drink?" she asks me.

"I'll have pineapple juice, please."

"Kiddie or adult size?" she asks.

I stare at her blankly and quickly realize how rude I'm being. But seriously, I'm twelve years old. A kiddie is way too small for me. Just as I'm about to say something, she seems to get it. "Adult it is," she says and turns to the other side of the table to take more orders.

I bite into my burger and let the juicy flavor sink into my tongue. Probably one of the most delicious burgers that I've ever eaten in my life. Okay, maybe eighteen dollars isn't so ridiculous. I look up and Cerel is literally admiring his burger. He's turning it over in his hand and looking at it in awe as he chews. With a mouthful he says, "Diff brrgrr iifs oh guud." I think he said his burger is so good. I nod in agreement.

Dad and Uncle Brygus talk about some doctor stuff and business...like most adults. Mom and Auntie Heather discuss how adorable baby Sara is while she sits on Hunter's lap. But I don't really find her cute right now, because she's got a bunch of boogies hanging out of her nose. Hunter sees this, too, but can't find any napkins. You'd think that a restaurant this expensive would have some napkins or tissues nearby...but nothing.

I end up finishing my burger much quicker than I thought I would. I'm still a bit hungry, but I already gave my fries to Armand, so I can't get them back. Once he's got something, he acts as if it's his territory, kind of like animals when they pee on their land to mark their place. Fortunately, he doesn't go that far. But with Dominic around, you never know.

I push my plate forward to show that I'm done eating and slouch a little bit so I can rest. People are always saying how slouching is rude and not good for you, but I think it feels great. I mean, I agree with the fact that it's rude and stuff. But when you're a kid, I think it's fine.

Armand and Dominic slide off the side of the couch and start rolling around the floor. Cerel sees them, looks at me, then at them, and back to me.

"What are they doing?" he asks me.

"I don't know, but it's really embarrassing."

We watch as the two of them keep falling all over each other. Cerel puts his hand in his hair and brushes it back from his face. He's clearly looking around again to see if anyone he knows is here, not wanting to be embarrassed.

"Any of your friends here?" I ask him.

"No…thank God."

Armand and Dominic start doing some weird dance-like thing that is…umm…how do I say this? Awkward? It just looks very wrong. It's kind of like The Worm dance, but more with the hips.

"What are you doing?" Cerel asks them.

"We're snailing!" Armand yells with a giddy smile. "You should try it!"

"I'll pass," Cerel says into his soda glass. At this point, our parents have had enough, and so have the people around us at the other tables. So Dad flags down the waitress, pays and hurries us out before we get asked to leave.

25

"I hate this show," Cerel complains to me. We're occupying baby Sara by sitting with her and watching Caillou on the Sprout Channel. "I didn't watch this stuff when I was little," Cerel mutters to me. "It's so…blah."

"Really?" I ask raising an eyebrow. "You didn't watch a single episode of-?"

Hunter storms through the room without looking at any of us, including his adorable little sister who's sitting in her sparkly pink bean bag chair. He just walks right past us and goes outside.

"What's with him?" I ask Cerel.

"I dunno," he replies with a shrug. "Who cares anyway?"

The show ends. Baby Sara jumps up and spins around in little circles. I love babies. They're so happy and adorable...except for the times when they start whining for something. Other than that, I do love them. THEY'RE SO PUDGY!

"So the ferry arrives in an hour," Uncle Brygus tells us as we sit around the picnic table with our bags by our feet. I look through mine to make sure I've got everything.

Books? Yup.

Clothes? Yup.

Hair brush and other bathroom stuff? Triple yup.

Do I have everything I need? Yup, yup, yup.

Armand and Dominic join everyone at the picnic table. "Armand's birthday is on Friday!" Dominic announces to the whole neighborhood. Across the table, Auntie Heather jumps up and runs into the house. As she does, Faegan sits next to his dad with a very confused look on his face, especially when she rushes out of the house with a sun hat on her head and the car keys in her hand.

"Where are you going?" Uncle Brygus asks.

"Shhh," Auntie Heather replies. "I'll tell you later."

Mom stands up. "Should I come with you?" she asks.

"No," Auntie Heather says, rushing toward the car. "It's okay, I'll go alone." Quickly, Auntie Heather jumps into the SUV and starts driving away with her door still open. Wow, she's in quite the rush. She pulls into the street, closes the door and gives a friendly beep of her horn as she darts out of the neighborhood.

"Well, that was strange," Uncle Brygus says to us. Then he looks at me. "So, did you enjoy your weekend here, Chloe?"

"Yes, I did. Thank you."

Armand realizes he never said thank you either, so he spits out a quick "Thank Youuuuuu!"

Cerel grunts and points to my dad who sits next to him. "I think they would have enjoyed the sailing part more if we didn't have to ride in a bathtub smaller than Sara's bed."

"Cerel," Uncle Brygus says quietly but in a frightening way. "You can stay here and appreciate what you have, or you may leave."

"I think I'll stay," Cerel says to his dad.

"Good," Uncle Brygus mutters under his breath. "Anyway, where was I before being rudely interrupted? What did you like about it, Chloe?"

Cerel snorts.

"Umm," I say, trying to think. "It was really fun. Ya know…the beach and stuff."

"Oh, come on!" Cerel says. "You don't have to lie."

"No, it was fun. Thank you," I say forcefully, because, it really has been.

"Psst, Chloe!" I hear someone whisper behind me. Startled, I turn around and find Auntie Heather standing there with two paper bags, one large and one small. "Don't tell your brother," she whispers to me as she begins pulling something out of the big bag. She slowly and carefully reveals a huge Oreo birthday cake. Yum! I want a piece.

"Is that for Armand?" I ask in a whisper. Nobody's out here, but I can see them close to the open windows overlooking where I sit.

"Oh, and this is for you, just in case when you're on the ferry for that full two hours," she says to me, as she pulls a pink box out of the smaller bag and - oh. I hope nobody comes out right now. I thought it would be like a pink box of mints or something, but it isn't. It's a box of feminine pads. Yes, pads. As in…those things.

"Oh, uh…thanks," I say. I'm surprised that she would get those for me. I fidget with my fingers, because this is kind of weird.

"It's okay," she says laughing. "When I was little, or, not when I was little. But anyway, I was in the bathroom and-"

"Do you want me to get some candles for that?" I ask quickly, pointing at the cake, before she can go on about the pads.

"I'll get the candles," she says. "You can go and find the others."

"Great!" I say and run off.

26

"**H**appy birthday to you, happy birthday to you!" everyone sings to Armand. When we're done singing, Auntie Heather cuts a piece of the cake. Dad and Uncle Brygus sip their iced teas and talk about nature...or at least, Uncle Brygus does. I don't think Dad's listening to a single word he's saying.

"WOO HOO!!!!" Armand and Dominic yell and start throwing frosting at each other by using their spoons as catapults.

Uncle Brygus checks his watch and stands up. "Guys! The ferry leaves in twenty minutes!"

That doesn't mean anything to Armand and Dominic. They keep on giggling and covering themselves in even more frosting.

"Dominic!" Uncle Brygus says in a scolding tone.

"Armand. Knock it off," Dad says.

Mom pulls some wet wipes out of her bag and swooshes a wipe all around Armand's face. Dominic runs away before Auntie Heather can do the same to him.

"Chloe," Dad says. "Can you put your stuff in the car?" I nod and grab my bags.

Walking to the car, I open the trunk and carefully put one bag inside, keeping the smaller one on my shoulder. I go back to the picnic table and find Cerel is now by himself and cutting a piece of cake.

"How ya doing'?" he asks, looking like he's trying to be cool.

"We literally just saw each other thirty seconds ago," I say.

Armand and Dominic run out of the house and jump into the car with everyone else following.

"Well, bye!" Cerel says to me. "Look out for those sharks."

"See ya," I say turning away. But I wait for a moment, "Oh, and don't forget to wash that beach shovel." Because like house guests, that thing's gonna start to stink after a few days.

END OF BOOK ONE

ACKNOWLEDGEMENTS

To the family with four boys and one darling little angel girl, I give a huge thank you for hosting one crazy weekend in the summer of 2014. Without your warmth and support, this book would never have been possible.

To my parents and brother. Thank you for loving me and having the patience to let me stay in my room for long hours each night without socializing at all.

To Dad for being a whole bunch of things, including my editor, agent, and PR guy. Your tireless support ensured that I could publish this first book in the series while still twelve years old.

To one of my dearest friends, Sarah O., for providing rapid review and commentary as the story progressed.

To Grandma and Papa, who cheered me on with numerous phone calls of encouragement, plus one very important edit.

To my cover designer, Caitlin Caudill, who captured my feelings in her work and even took my call during her St. Patrick's day party.

ABOUT THE AUTHOR

Without a doubt, my top three favorite things are sleeping in, watching movies and reading books. To me, there's nothing better than waking up at eleven on a Saturday morning to the sight of snow falling outside my window. When I write, I need some background noise, because silence scares me almost as much as clowns do. Other than being a couch potato, I love spending time and goofing around with my friends. They crack me up.

Connect with me online:
Tumblr: citratenore.tumblr.com
Web: www.citratenore.com